T0065539

AIN'T NO
PLACE SAFE

CARLITO EWELL

authorHOUSE®

AuthorHouse™
1663 Liberty Drive
Bloomington, IN 47403
www.authorhouse.com
Phone: 1 (800) 839-8640

Published by AuthorHouse 08/25/2016

ISBN: 978-1-5246-1716-5 (sc)
ISBN: 978-1-5246-1717-2 (hc)
ISBN: 978-1-5246-1715-8 (e)

Library of Congress Control Number: 2016910880

Print information available on the last page.

Any people depicted in stock imagery provided by Thinkstock are models, and such images are being used for illustrative purposes only. Certain stock imagery © Thinkstock.

This book is printed on acid-free paper.

Because of the dynamic nature of the Internet, any web addresses or links contained in this book may have changed since publication and may no longer be valid. The views expressed in this work are solely those of the author and do not necessarily reflect the views of the publisher, and the publisher hereby disclaims any responsibility for them.

Dedication

To Dr. John Kovach at Chestnut Hill College in Philadelphia PA. Your hard work on all of my writings as well as your commitment to me as a friend could never be repaid. I thank you and wish only peace and prosperity at your door step.

Carlton "Carlito" Ewell

Day One

Raheem held his cousin's head close to his chest, his face felt the prickle of Kareem's closely cut hair. He was rocking back and forth with a thousand yard stare as a crowd began to form around them.

"We got two more summers, Reem, then we are out Cuz," Raheem was saying the words but there was no response. "What do you think, man? Tar Heels or UCLA? Yeah, yeah, I know, you look good in that Georgetown jacket. I ain't playing for no team in D.C. and that's that, Cuz."

The crowd had now swelled to around 30 and the sounds of sirens from the police and ambulance were coming closer.

Both Raheem and Kareem lay in a puddle of Kareem's blood. Neither one had on sneakers as they were crouched at the edge of the local basketball court. It was clear to all what had just taken place. Both young boys had become victims to the ever growing trend; sneaker robberies. Raheem had given his "Jordans" up almost immediately when he saw the nine mill. The other players ran like rabbits, including Kareem. The gunman simply shot him in the back and one of the other accomplices ran toward the center of the once sacred ground and removed Kareem's fresh new "Runs."

"Everybody back, get back, you wanna go to jail for murder?" The emotionless officer said to no one in particular.

"Look at this shit," the cop said, now talking to his partner while looking down at the two young men.

"Come on son, let me help you." The young twenty-something white male said as another medic tended to Kareem. "Are you hurt? Have you been shot?"

Raheem never responded, he simply watched with tunnel vision as the now four paramedics worked frantically to revive his lifeless fifteen year old cousin that lay on the court.

After several minutes, the medics placed the limp body of Kareem Porter onto a rolling gurney and pushed him through the somber crowd, into the waiting open back door of the ambulance.

"At least they didn't put him in the meat wagon," one middle-aged woman said to a group of older on-lookers. "Damn, he was fine, why they kill him?" A young teenaged girl said to a few other girls dressed in short skirts and midriff exposing tight tube tops.

"I heard it was over his new Jordans," one of the girls said as they all watched as the ambulance door was slammed shut.

A dazed Raheem was led to an unmarked police car, driven by the local good cop, bad cop homicide team of "Tom and Jerry." Two real-life cartoon characters, Detective Tom Galinsky and Jerald Ondreka. They were the only homicide detectives in the City of Philadelphia with a 90 percent case closure rate. The problem with that 90 percent was that 80 percent of the men that they fingered were innocent! It didn't matter, this was the "Badlands," the 25th Police District. A large community, mixed with Blacks, Latinos, poor Irish whites, Pitbulls, prostitutes, drug dealers and heroin.

To the police, especially the homicide unit, there were no good young men in the "Badlands." So, as far as Tom and Jerry were concerned, Kareem was just a statistic, and sooner or later somewhere down the road, they would be on the hunt for Raheem.

"Those Goddamn Flyers blew a third period lead again," Tom yelled to break the silence in the ragged vehicle, a clear sign of how tight the City budget was year after year. Each day the two detectives climbed into their "hoop-dee." They longed for the days when the city and its officials placed the police department at the top of the budget and not at the tail.

"City Council all got new cars and so did Parking," Tom would mutter.

"Parking got new vehicles too?" Gerald always sounded surprised even though he'd heard Tom mention this fact many times.

"Yeah, I heard they wanted the City to look good while giving out parking tickets. Meanwhile, we're driving around in a taxi cab."

"Frank would never stand for it. He's gotta be turning over in his grave," Tom would say of the say of former Mayor and Police Chief Frank Rizzo.

"If Big Frank were alive we'd have new vehicles, I'll tell you dat," Jerry cried each day like a prayer.

The detectives drove a young Raheem to Philadelphia's infamous "Round House." The Roundhouse was the City's Police Headquarters which was built in the mid-1960s. It was, indeed, round, but even with its mid-century modern exterior, it was a mess from the opening day.

"Come on, Kareem," Jerry said as he opened the back door of the old dick car from the outside.

"I'm Raheem, Kareem is dead," a very soft-spoken Raheem said without the slightest hint of anger or sarcasm. Neither his voice nor his mannerisms matched his six foot-five frame or his huge hands and feet. Unlike Kareem, Raheem was very humble and subdued. Kareem knew he was a highly sought after division one-A college recruit and he wore it on his sleeve. Although Raheem was also just as aggressively recruited, he refused to dream past today's task at hand.

A shoeless Raheem walked gingerly into police headquarters to look at mug shots and answer questions. It didn't take very long before the madness began.

"Come on, man, you know who shot your cousin, you and your homies want to handle it your way, right?" Tom, now was playing the bad guy.

"It happen real fast, plus I'm not from sixth and Master; I don't know the guys around there," Raheem calmly said as he looked at his now filthy, once bleached white socks.

"Where are you from, what corner do you hustle on?" Jerry's tone showed that he was trying to be nice and gain some trust.

"Hustle? I go to school, I don't hustle,"

Both cops burst out in laughter as if the young man had said something truly amusing. "School? Come on, cut it the fuck out kid. We're being nice here, give us a lead," Tom interjected.

"We were just looking for some good rec so we decided on 6th and Master because we heard Munchie was gonna be there," Raheem quietly said without breaking in his word."

"What gang is Munchie from?" One of the detectives quickly responded.

"Munchie ain't in no gang, he plays for a team overseas...Turkey or Italy I think. He's just home for a break in their season. Sometimes he plays pick up on his home court with guys from around his way." Raheem continued to keep his composure even though he found these two detectives to be totally clueless.

"Oh okay, so he's from 6th and Master?"

"Yeah but," Raheem was quickly interrupted.

"He's the one who set this whole hit up then, right?"

"What?"

"Did you and Raheem owe him money?"

"Kareem, I'm Ra..."

"How much did you owe him."

"We ain't owe money," Raheem now began to sound more agitated.

"Don't get tough wit me punk! I'll mash your got damn head through that wall."

Raheem's eyes were now wide open and his mouth agape. He was aware of the police brutality in his community but had never experience it himself. He could now add "fear of police" to his list of recent life-changing experiences.

Just then the interrogation room door opened up.

"Tom, Jerry," a police Lieutenant detective called in. The two detectives stepped outside the room.

"Yeah, Bob," Tom said. "The kid's grandmother is over there," the Lieutenant said as he nodded and looked across the room. "She's with some local preacher also; the show's over boys." The Lieutenant added, "Be nice, got me?" The Lieutenant looked at both of his detectives with a very stern stare and walked away...

Chapter 1

Raheem Porter, fifteen years old, very tall, fair complexion, with cocoa brown colored eyes and jet black hair. Raheem, along with his sixteen year old sister, two female cousins, one sixteen and one fifteen and now deceased cousin Kareem, all neatly crammed into their grandmother's old brick three bedroom row house on the corner of 9th and Indiana streets.

The notorious 9th and Indi. Famously called the Badlands. Mother Porter's house sat directly across from an old pet cemetery that was in constant use by transient heroin addicts. The entire four corner block was an open air market for dope. The dope in Philadelphia during the 1980s and 1990s was considered the most addictive when compared to the other major cities across America. Daily, hundreds of beautiful young women fell victim to the needle. After becoming a slave to the deadly brew, most all young women began to trick in one form or another.

Mother Porter's house was no different when it came to being victimized. She had first lost her husband in 1978 to an overdose. After successfully raising two sons as a single mother under an extremely tough set of circumstances, both of her daughters fell in love with the "Witch Doctor." Each daughter had somehow birthed healthy children.

Lisa, had three and Dundee (Raheem's mother) had two. Both the whereabouts as well as exactly who was the father of these children was always in question. In Raheem's case, it was anyone's guess. Both Lisa and Dundee had been tricking before they became pregnant with each child. Dundee, however, always claimed that Raheem's father was an NBA player she was secretly dating before she had become pregnant with him in 1990, shortly after the death of their grandfather. Although the story of the NBA player was never confirmed, the fact that both Raheem and Kareem were the only tall men in the entire family line to stand over six feet-two, begged the question of the possibility that the two may even have been fathered by the same man. They were practically twins, both born one month after the other during a time when the two sisters were in the street...

One Month Later--May 2000

"Good morning, Nana," Raheem quietly said from behind the curtain that separated the laundry room from the front of the basement where Raheem had his bedroom. This space had been shared with his cousin before he was killed.

"Good morning, Baby," Mother Porter replied as she loaded the washer with the first of many loads for the day. "Your breakfast is ready," she quietly uttered without looking up from the washing machine.

Raheem stood up from the large clean mattress that was thrown on the floor without a box spring, bed frame or even top sheets. He slid the sheer curtain to one side. Towering over his grandmother, he bent down and kissed his Nana on the left cheek and walked up the steps into the small kitchen.

The air was full of the unmistakable smell of pork bacon, grits smothered in grated yellow cheese and butter, scrambled eggs with toast.

It was a welcoming scent. Mother Porter always found a way to feed her babies very well. She had made it a point that there would always be breakfast and dinner, no matter what it took to provide.

Raheem sat down in front of his cousin Kia and began to pile his plate with the morning fare.

"Where's Keisha and Keema?" Raheem asked as he was scooping a mouth full of both scrambled cheese eggs mixed with the buttery grits.

"Keema left for school early," Kia said with a wink. "And Keisha pulled another all-nighter with Tito; Nana is gonna kill her." Kia continued to finish her breakfast.

"She gone end up pregnant, I bet you," Raheem said as he poured himself a glass of cold orange juice.

"No she ain't, Nana got us all Depro shots last month; she said we the last kids she raising."

"Yeah, but that don't give yall reason to run around givin it up," Raheem said as he began plate number two.

"I ain't givin nothing up, I'm a virgin. Nana still made me get the shot anyway," Kia said as she began to clear up some of the empty plates.

"I might have to talk to Tito when I see him, "Raheem stated with a firm tone.

"Fool, you can't stop love, love rules," Kia shot back as she was now washing a few plates and stacking them neatly beside the sink.

"Tito don't love no girls, he just runs through them."

"Not Tito, Keema!" Kia said with a look of disgust because her brother just wasn't getting it.

Breakfast ended just as abruptly as it had begun. Raheem grabbed his black back pack with his school stuff at the sound of the car horn outside. It was his two friends, Bo and Moop, the front court of his high school basketball team. Both Bo and Moop were seniors and headed to big time basketball schools at the end of the summer. They had all of their credits to graduate so the last 30 days of school was just time to hang out with their younger team mates and to pick up girls.

"Young boy, what's happening," A hyped Bo yelled over the blaring sounds of "Cash Money." Raheem gave each friend a pound as he got comfortable in the back seat of Bo's brand new SUV, complements of his Uncle by way of a college booster happy that the star guard would be attending his alma mater in Cincinnati.

"How you like my new whip," Bo yelled over the next tune.

"It's all that Booster Money," Raheem responded.

"I get mine in a week. We had to have my neighbor sign for it Cuz; I'm a be pushin a Lincoln truck when I get to N.C. State," Moop was smiling ear to ear as he spoke those words.

Bo turned the system down a bit and asked Raheem, "You good Heem? You know about Reem? I know it's tough, but he would want the best for you. You sixteen in a few days and colleges is kickin your door down. We got you on the lil change for sneaks and stuff, and my man Snooky told me that some dudes from 17th Street is on them dudes top about some other robberies as well as Reem."

4

"I ain't on it like that," Raheem shrugged his shoulders as he responded. "Like Nana said, they gone get theirs no matter what."

The three ballers pulled up to Thomas Edison High School. Everyone in the parking lot was looking to see who was in the shiny new SUV. There were so many new cars in the parking lot it was hard to tell which were the staff and which belonged to the students. The warm weather had the girls dressing more risqué than usual. As the crew parked and got out, girls swarmed the trio like bees.

"Heem, why you ain't call me?" One short Dominican girl said with her left arm holding her one composition book and her right hand on her hip.

"Was I supposed to?" Raheem asked as he grabbed his bag out of the back of the truck.

"I told you I was try to see you about something," giving Raheem a look as if he should have known.

"Oyeah, I had to study for my calculus final, plus my Grandma wanted me home early."

"Your Grandmom wanted you home early?" The girl yelled in disbelief.

Raheem just walked off at the sound of the first bell as if the girl wasn't there.

"We be back at the let out, Heem," Bo yelled as he opened the back door to his new truck to allow two girls in before pulling off...

Chapter 2

"And what does the battle between the White Whale and Captain Ahab represent to you? That was the question for your final paper, class. Is anyone willing to volunteer or is anyone brave enough to give the class an opportunity to hear and discuss your objective opinion of the reading of Herman Melville's classic *Moby Dick*?" The tall skinny white male of middle-age asked his class in a stoic professor-like manner. One young lady raised her hand.

"Yes, Ms Reeves."

"The Captain was mad at all the whales in the sea because he lost his leg to one when he was a young man. Now he was getting back at them by killing the big white whale." The young lady smiled when she completed her answer and sat down.

"What do you have to say to Ms Reeves' answer, class?" The teacher asked and waited for an answer. Most of the class was going about their own quiet business of note-passing as well as having separate conversations, even one or two had laid their heads down to doze off for the 45 minutes of English Literature class.

"How about you, Mr. Pitts, since you're having a conference in the back of the room; what might you say to Ms Reeve's answer?"

"Who me?"

"Yes, you are Mr. Pitts aren't you?" The teacher said with a condescending tone.

"Oh, yeah, yeah, well, all I can say is Moby had a real big dick, Reeves should know that!" The entire room broke out in laughter.

"Out Mr. Pitts, and don't bother leaving at dismissal, you bought yourself one detention." The teacher was struggling to maintain his composure as he spoke.

"And I got a real big dick too," the boy said as he closed the door to the classroom that was now filled with laughter once more.

"Mr. Pitts will be attending summer school for all who would like to join him." The teacher continued, "Okay, can anyone elaborate on the inner meaning? How about you Mr. Porter." The teacher was standing in the row and right beside him.

"Do I have to stand up?" A sly sounding Raheem said.

"No, you do not, but please speak up."

"Well, I disagree with the thinking of a fight between Ahab and the white whale. I think the fight was deep inside of Ahab himself and the author, Melville, used the whale as well as the color of the whale as a symbol of a greater fight within himself."

The teacher just looked at Raheem in total silence. "Where did you come up with such an answer Mr. Porter, have you read anything else by Herman Melville to help you come to such a conclusion?"

"I don't know anything about the author, but I do know about inner struggle and I definitely know about outer struggle; I live in the *Land*," a very calm but quietly confident Raheem spoke without a hint of second guessing himself.

"Very good," the teacher was now smiling himself. After the bell had rung and the students were handing in their papers as they filed out, Mr. Prescott, Raheem's English Lit teacher, stopped him as he began to leave.

"Hold on Mr. Porter," Mr. Prescott said in a warm, soft tone. "I am really, really impressed with your growth this year. Your papers are thorough and complete. Your insight is deep and mature. I was particularly impressed with your view of George Orwell's *Animal Farm*. How are you coming up with such strong analogical opinions at your age?" Mr. Prescott spoke with a look of wonder on his face.

Raheem's eyes and brows came together as if he were studying what was just said by his teacher, then he spoke. "What's analogical?"

"It's where you make the logical argument parallel to something else, possibly even another subject," the teacher said while watching Raheem's strong, quiet confidence.

"Yeah, well, I read the work and then I think about it, then I think about my life, my cousin, my neighborhood. Somehow, it always fits; I have a hard time finding the words, but my Grandmother got us a computer and that has helped a lot." Raheem finished and somehow at that very moment he just understood how he was able to comprehend and write such good papers. He felt really good about his work; he had put forth a great deal of effort into his papers as well as his studies in his junior year and good things were truly beginning to happen because of this hard work.

As the day moved on, class after class, final after final, each teacher was pulling Raheem to the side to compliment him on his steep progress. Raheem had finally made the correlation that if he worked as hard on his school work as he had done with basketball fundamentals, he could become a very good student also. In fact, now that he had obtained all As in his finals, he surmised that next year, as a senior, he could possibly get straight As. "Straight As," Raheem thought, "Wow," none of his basketball friends ever talked about straight As, in truth, they never spoke about any As. They never completed papers or finals. "Girls did everything for star ball players in each sport, in every high school in Philly; that's' just the way it is," Raheem now in deep thought about his new mission...

Later that afternoon, Raheem was picked up in the parking lot by Bo and Moop. The trio as well as two more street-ball teammates were headed to an indoor pick-up game about 45 minutes away in Tom's River, New Jersey. Since the murder of Kareem in broad daylight, and the rash of robberies for top-of-the-line sneakers, the young b-ball crews turned to more indoor rec and out of the way basketball courts in the burbs. Most of the competition was sub-par, with the exception of the small college all white teams from surrounding schools. Raheem had learned that the white boys are always fundamentally sound on the court. They played a smart steady game.

"Who we playin Yo?" Raheem asked his older friend Bo, now 18 years of age and increasingly filling in on his role as team leader.

"Some dudes from Monmouth University. They ain't really that good in DI-A, but in pick up they sometimes get Chocolate Thunder to play center; he lives just up the road from the gym." Bo started fishing around on his CD changer for some Jay-Z.

"Who," Raheem asked.

"Chocolate Thunder, Daryl Dawkins, man."

"Who is that?" The young Raheem asked truly not knowing the former Sixer.

"He was our All Star center back in the day," Moop schooled the young small forward/guard.

"Our, our who? I'm a later in life dude and Kareem Abdul-Jabbar was my All Star Center," Raheem yelled over Jay-Z's sound of "The Blue Print."

As the five ball players walked into the expensive indoor facility with top flight equipment, Raheem was the only member of the crew who was awestruck about how nice and new everything was. The gym floor was hard, glossy, well-waxed wood, the back boards were Plexiglas, and all the on-court lines were freshly painted. Raheem noticed how the adults at the front desk and the women running on treadmills behind a large window watched their every move.

"Yo, Bo, are we allowed in here, all those people are watching us," Raheem whispered.

"Fool, we Black, and we all over six-five, they know what the deal is and they probably think we pros," Bo shot back with an air of pride. At the opposite side of the gymnasium stood eight young men. Six white and two Black. They all looked to be in their early twenties. They too stood over six-five to six-nine, save the lone point guard, Travis Kurtz who was the North East Conference's reigning scoring and assist champ. Travis and Bo were friendly rivals from summer AAU camps and games up and down the Eastern Seaboard.

"How are you, Bo?" Travis offered his right hand and shook with a hug from his left.

"I'm good, man, how about you?" Bo responded. All the rest of the Monmouth team were shaking hands and lightly chatting with their much younger competition.

"Cincy, huh? I couldn't convince you to come to the little white boy school, huh?" Travis said jokingly.

"You know me, Trav, I like bright lights and big parties. If I came with you over to Monmouth, they might expect me to actually come to class every day," Bo said and all the ballers with Travis fell out laughing.

"That's true, and I hate it," one of the bigger athletes piped in.

"Enough chit-chat; we got a running clock and one ref. We play two forty minute games against each other, then you and I pick teams from all of us and we play two more games; good enough?" Travis was clearly a business major.

With that, all the guys had a very brief warm up and then tipped off. Bo was at the point guard position playing man-on the shorter Travis. Moop was the three position at power forward, Malik was at center, being the tallest at six-ten, and Raheem played a slash shooting guard, small forward. Last was Mill, who was also a very big six-eight 260 pounds; he played forward.

Malik won the tip, and shot the rock to Bo. Bo, having played with Raheem at least a thousand times knew the drill as he took off toward the basket like a rocket. He simply lobbed the ball in the near vicinity of the basket. While the opposing college players watched what they assumed was an errant pass, a super athletic Raheem caught the ball at its peak and dunked it with the authority of a man with six years in the NBA.

"Two-nothing, the high school kids, I told you guys that they're fast; I told you that they're very fast," Travis coached his team as they brought the ball in bounds.

The college team was just as Bo had said, very fundamentally sound and methodical. With their lack of foot speed, the other players used the speed of the pass.

"Nobody's faster than the ball," Travis yelled, after a six pass two point shot from the left side of the baseline.

A quick in-bound, and Raheem was back at it. "Stop and pop. Pick him up at half court, don't try to press him he's too fast," Travis yelled to the out-matched player from the college team. This went on for several exchanges. The high speed above the rim play from Bo and Raheem vs. the slow-footed, quick ball movement from Travis and company. After the first 40 minutes the buzzer rang and the score was 45 to 40 for the high school team.

Travis quickly subbed two players for two quicker guys that were much smaller in weight than Malik and Mill. The pay-off was almost immediate. Travis backed his entire team up on D and played a 2-3 zone against the super kids. "Everybody stay put; make them beat us with the three," a quick adjusted Travis yelled. It worked; shot after shot. Not one three ball landed. The hard foul sent the big bodied Malik to the line like "Hack a Shaq" Boink, their big men just couldn't shoot foul shots. In fact, if not for easy layups or dunks, the big men for the city kids couldn't buy a basket.

This did not go unnoticed by a very observant Travis. "You box out before he gets inside the key," the intense Travis yelled. It was clear that Travis was determined to win. He shouted at the ref for two missed calls, "Just give the game away, why don't cha?"

Bo had finally had enough, "Time Out. Listen," Bo said as all five of the young ballers walked toward the water fountain. "Let's play a three guard set, but Heem, you bring the ball up court and I'll run Travis around the baseline, when they go to double, you up on the cut, I'll dump off to Mill for an easy dunk. We will do that twice, then again off the screen. Once they pick it up, Heem shoot the mid-range jumper. Come on man, we should be killing these white boys, they out thinkin us." Bo finally finished.

"You guys need an invite or what? We been waiting forever," a smart-mouthed Travis yelled across the gym.

Mill in-bound the ball to Raheem who quickly dribbled across half court. Raheem chest-passed the ball to Moop at the left side of the baseline, Moop bounce-passed the ball to Malik at the top of the key and Malik gave Bo a behind the back pass right as he was running under the rim for a reverse lay-up.

"Nobody is faster than the ball," Bo yelled at Travis as all five hurried to get back. Travis ignored Bo as he in-bound. Travis was now acting as if he were tired while now playing the two-guard. The act didn't last long as the quick passes to all five players ended with Travis squaring up for the long three. *Swish!*

"Man I'm tired," Travis complained.

"Yeah right," Bo said feeling challenged. Bo came right back and faked a three and threw the ball to high flying Raheem for a reverse dunk. The very humble Raheem simply jogged back up court. The entire gym was now sparsely filled with on-lookers. Unlike the city gyms where only neighborhood kids hang out, this place had all types. Businessmen and women, swim team guys some volley ball players and weight lifters, you name it. It became a real show. With 15 seconds left the score was 55-58 in game two for the college team.

Bo resumed his position at the point. He crossed half court, passed the ball to Raheem who immediately passed to Mill in the middle; Mill hit Malik and Malik passed out to Raheem for the three that would tie the game. Raheem was open and squared up. He rose two-and-a-half feet off the floor for a perfect stroke but the ball went hard off the back of the rim. Baaaam! The buzzer sounded. One-one, the college kids had saved face. The crowd looked in awe at the very young kids because of their athletic ability.

The rest of the afternoon was mixed play, just pure fun watching Raheem and his fancy high flying act. Travis and his motor-mouth added a spicy commentary to the game making it fun for all. After a light snack with the Travis team and some soft drinks, the two teams said their goodbyes with the promise of meeting up in a few weeks. The kids from the city began their drive home. Just as they were beginning to talk about how good the day had been, reality struck!

At first, Bo thought the New Jersey State Troopers lights were for another vehicle and would drive right past. But after the siren sounded and the Trooper yelled "Pull over" on the vehicle microphone, he and the other four kids piled in the back of the shiny new Cadillac Escalade realized that they were the target. Bo immediately complied.

"Was up, man?" Malik quietly asked.

"I don't know, just be cool, we ain't did nothing wrong," Bo quickly taking charge.

"Turn the truck off and toss the keys out the window on the road," The Trooper stated clearly over the loud speaker. Bo immediately complied. His left arm remained out the driver side window waiting for the next command. Five minutes passed by, then ten. One more Trooper pulled up and then two more. One happened to be a K-9 unit.

"What the hell," Bo quietly complained to no one in particular. All four Troopers surrounded the vehicle with a large German Shepherd extended at the leash. He was barking and gnashing his large teeth. The Trooper at Raheem's door opened it.

"Get all your fuckin hands in the air." Each kid was well over six feet tall so their arms bent at the ceiling. Each boy was visibly shaken as he was removed from the SUV, cuffed behind his back and placed face down in the grass on the side of the road. With the ferocious K-9 snarling and barking mere inches from each boy's ears, the head Trooper asked, "Why are you so nervous? Where are the guns? Where are the drugs? You want me to let Trooper Max go? He'll eat your big black ass, boy."

The large Shepherd now was millimeters from Mill's crotch. "If you move I swear I'll let him go," Max's handler yelled over the barking and passing traffic.

"We was playing basketball, Sir," Mill cried out.

This went on for over 30 minutes as the State Troopers tore Bo's shiny new SUV apart looking for drugs and guns. There wasn't a sign of either. A quick check of each ID came up spotless. The truck was clean also.

With faces in the grass, the cuffs came off. No one dared to move. Finally the barking came to a halt. One after the next, the boys could hear the gravel between the ground and the tires. After what seemed like eternity, the five young men gained the courage to slowly get up one-by-one. Bo saw his new SUV and tears quietly streamed down his face. The same for Moop and Malik. Mill was trying to hold back tears but it just wouldn't happen. Both he and Raheem started to quietly join in with the obvious expression of their hurt.

On the long quiet ride home, there was no Jay-Z or Tupac nor Biggie. Just the loud sound of silence. A beautiful day in a New Jersey suburb away from the violence of the Band Lands proved to be not so beautiful after all.

Chapter 3

"You got mail from a few colleges," Mother Porter said as Raheem walked into the house.

"Thanks, Nana," Raheem walked into the small dining room that was a mere 10 feet by 10 feet box. Just large enough to hold a small table and chairs. He picked up the mail and entered the kitchen greeting Mother Porter with a kiss on the cheek.

"Go wash up, Nana made your favorite," Mother Porter softly said as she checked on the butter-milk biscuits in the oven. The air in the small house was thick and heavy with the smell of both fired and baked foods. Mother Porter grabbed another oven mitt and lifted the lid to the large iron pot with her left hand and slowly stirred the stewed chicken and dumplings with her right. There were two pies on the kitchen table contributing to the welcoming aroma wafting through the house. One was peanut butter crunch, her family's South Carolina recipe from as far back as the Jim Crow South's beginning, and one apple. Lastly, Mother Porter would fry up some wings with hot sauce on the side, along with the collard greens cooked in smoked turkey butts. Each night, Mother cooked like this. First to eat would be Raheem after a game or practice. Next would be his youngest cousin Kia. Usually his sister Keema would eat with Kia and Keisha's hot tail would always be last. Lately with

Tito on her trail, she was missing Mother's meals and curfews with increasing frequency.

After Mother made sure that all the children ate each night, she would take in the orders from Tito's workers on the corner. Mother Porter charged $7.50 a plate and one dollar for lemonade or sweet tea. She did this seven days a week; on weekends she also added white potato and sweet potato pie. The white potato pie became so popular, she and Kia spent all day Saturday preparing pies. Even the local narcotic cops began to ask about her pies. Tito's drug gang loved Mother Porter's food, but she never had more than ten extra plates and once the food was gone, that was it until the following day. This, and the few loads of laundry that Mother Porter did for some customers from her old days of housekeeping, was all the income that came into the Porter house. Some government food stamps, but that was it. Mother's cooking on the weekend took care of all the bills in one fell swoop. The rest was saved, some in Mother's savings account at the same bank on Germantown and Lehigh Avenues where she had been banking and saving for 30 years. The extras were for both Kareem and Raheem's basketball sneakers; sadly now only Raheem would need shoes. The girl's clothing was much cheaper and easier to purchase right on the Avenue.

"Who wrote to you?" Mother Porter asked Raheem as he stuffed an entire biscuit in his hungry teenaged mouth. With strawberry jam on his chin, he reached for three wings with his one large hand.

"UConn and St. John's," Raheem said as Mother Porter handed him a white paper towel. Now eating the wings with hot sauce and shoveling baked macaroni and cheese in his mouth, Mother asked, "Where is St. John's?"

"It's in New York City," Raheem replied as Mother took one plate away and replaced it with a large bowl full of chicken and dumplings.

She smiled with amazement at how her baby knew about big colleges all over the country.

"Nana, I don't like either one of them," Raheem said as an afterthought.

"Yeah, well them folks is gonna pay for your college, boy, then you surely pickin one of these people who been writing."

"I know, Nana, I will. I'll make some visits to a few schools next year." Raheem was now starting on his first piece of pie.

Just then, Keisha walked into the house.

"You still live here?" Raheem said between forks of his pie.

"Real funny, boy, hi Nana," Keisha was smiling broadly as she kissed her on the cheek.

"Eat girl, then get started on these pots for me."

Keema came bouncing down the steps. "Why you trying Nana, girl?" Keema spoke directly to Keisha in a semi-whisper.

"I ain't trying her," Keisha responded. The rest of the meal was, in fact, uneventful, but Raheem knew sooner or later, Mother Porter and Keisha would be having "the talk." More sooner than later.

"Cmon Kia and help me get these two pies out of the oven," Mother Porter bluntly stated. "I have enough food for 12 full platters tonight!"

"Nana, I need money for my summer clothes," Keema said at the thought of extra money being made from Mother Porter's platters.

"Then you had better start helping out around here. Right now the only one who's earned any money for clothes is Kia."

"I help, Nana, I help out all the time," Keema interjected.

"I'm gonna say this once; I got two extra laundry jobs and the summer is coming. I'll need all the help I can get with the night time platters. If you want to have money for the summer, then I suggest that you start helping me out more," Mother Porter announced.

"I always help, Nana," Kia said.

"I ain't talking to you Little One." Mother Porter always called Kia that name because of her petite sized. "I'm talking to these two." Now Mother was pointing to both Keema and Keisha.

Just then, there was a knock at the door. Keisha and Keema both rushed to answer it, almost knocking each other down in their hurry.

"Was up, June," Keema said to the teenaged light-skinned boy dressed like a rapper with skinny jeans, tight shirt, and lots of jewelry announcing his presence.

"Was up, Keema," the young man said while staring at Keema's very shapely body and then finally raising his eyes to meet hers with a bit of a blush.

"What you want?" Keema responded as if he was there to see her and she was beginning to play hard to get.

"I'm here for platters and stuff."

"And stuff, what you mean?" Keema now had her hand on her right hip.

"Cmon girl, you always giving me a hard time."

"Come in, June," Keisha yelled over her sister's shoulder.

"Hi Mother Porter," the polite young man said.

"Hi June, how many yall want?" Mother responded while beginning to prepare plates.

"Tito said as many as you can make and two whole pies, please," June responded. Mother Porter carefully prepared each plastic plate with heaping portions of southern style fare while Kia piled extra plates with rolls and cold potato salad.

"You gonna need help with this, June," Mother stated.

"I got plenty of help, Mother Porter, I just need to get the food to the step." June then grabbed as much food as he could and walked back to the frame door. Once he stepped outside the sweet young boy transformed immediately into his street role.

"Yo, cmon, come grab this shit!" The teenaged boy now in his role as shift manager of the heroin corner. "Tell them I said come get this food and don't eat shit till me or Tito get over there." June was speaking to the much older man in similar clothing, just not as tight. After all of the food and drinks were sent to the corner, June turned back to the living room, "How much we owe Mother?"

For the food platters, that's one-hundred and the pies, that's fourteen and the drinks is twenty. That' $134, Honey," Mother quickly said. The young man dug into his back pocket and unfolded several one-hundred dollar bills, peeled off two.

"Keep the change, Mother," as he handed her the money.

"Thank-you, baby," Mother quietly said as she stuck the folded bills down into her bra.

"Bye June," Keema said as he exited...

Chapter 4

The end of the school year is a season welcomed by just about everyone. Students, teachers, the city zoo and recreational parks such as Six Flags are all glad to see the summer begin. In fact, parents are probably the only group that doesn't welcome the summer. Most parents see the transition to summer as time off for the schools that they can use as a seven hour-a-day sitter for their children. Once the summer begins, they must find other ways to keep their teenagers busy throughout the long hot days.

For Mother Porter, keeping her girls out of trouble wasn't much of a challenge until their bodies began to mature. Now it had become a daily struggle with school in or out. As far as Raheem, she knew where he would be each day--on the basketball court or in a gym. As long as Raheem wasn't standing on the corner of 9th and Indiana selling heroin, Mother Porter felt a sense of safety concerning her grandson's whereabouts. That was up until the murder of her eldest grandson, Kareem. Now, until Raheem called to check in or walked through the front door, Mother Porter was in constant worry all summer.

Summer, 2001:

Just as New York has its Rucker Park in the summer for its elite ballers, Philadelphia's hollowed grounds are in North Philly, just a stone's throw away from Temple University. The summer league at 16th and Susquehanna Streets was set up by several members in the AAU basketball community but it wasn't recognized as part of the AAU in any official manner. In fact, 16th Street league breaks all the AAU rules. Age limit–none; sponsorship–anyone with money! This always leads to the city's major drug lords financing the best teams. The winner simply claims bragging rights.

In the case of Raheem and his friends, they were a team that simply entered the league without a benefactor.

"We need $500 this year to play," Bo said to Raheem.

"Five hundred, why so much?" To Raheem, this seemed like a mountain of money.

"I don't know, maybe the refs want more, plus Power 99 will be on hand, college recruits, as well as some pro scouts," Bo responded but was visibly discouraged himself.

"I have money but I'm holding out for school."

"I know." Bo continued, "Big Scratch ask me to put a team together last season, maybe he will sponsor us this year."

"If that's the case, why not just have each player come up with one hundred a piece; why should we give an outside sponsor the credit if we win the chip?" Raheem questioned.

"Yeah, but we'll each need at least four pairs of runs (sneakers) to get through the entire league play as well as uniforms. We gotta be lookin fresh for the crowd," Bo had seen fit to push the matter as the two drove down Second Street toward Girard to meet up with some street ballers in the Northern Liberties section of the city.

What else is good with you?" Bo asked his younger friend and team mate.

"I don't know, I'm a bit bummed out about ball lately," Raheem said.

"How so, Heem?" Bo's face twisted with a quizzical look.

"I mean, I love the rock and all, but don't you want to go to school for something else?" Raheem sounded like he'd been thinking about this for a while.

"Something else? What else?" Bo now turned the radio completely off to suggest that this talk had just turned serious.

"I mean like, maybe law or science, I don't know," Raheem was trying to explain himself but was finding it increasingly difficult.

"Law, science, all that's more work than it's worth, man; I'm headed to the League," Bo said with conviction.

"Yeah that's what I mean; what if you don't make the League, then what?" Raheem was becoming a more motivated speaker.

"Then what? Ain't no then what! I'm going pro no matter what. Either the NBA or at the very least–and it aint' gonna happen–but at the least, the European leagues. They always want us." Bo was sounding very clear and convincing.

"You got it all mapped out, huh Bo," Raheem said as his voice tapered off thinking about his cousin Kareem. Kareem had it all worked out also and look at how easily his dream was snatched away from him in a flash.

Reem's life was now just a mere memory that hovered in Raheem's mind on a daily basis. How Raheem missed his bragging charismatic cousin.

"You hear me, Reem?" Bo yelled.

"Yeah I hear you," Raheem said but didn't hear him at all.

The two pulled up to a neighborhood gym at 4th street and Fairmount Avenue. There they were met by the rest of their team as well as the "Northern Liberty Ballers" that consisted of older--over 30--ballers including a 40-something year old baller by the name of Blair Floyd. Floyd was old enough to have fathered each member of Raheem's team but he was also still in tip-top shape and had maintained his magnificent ball skills. Although Floyd had never made it to the NBA, the six foot two-inch point guard was just as good as anybody during his prime.

"What's up youngan, how you been?" Floyd said to Raheem as he extended his right hand to shake.

"Hey Mr. Floyd," a polite Raheem answered.

"Cmon man, I'm not that old am I?" Everyone in the group erupted into laughter!

"You old enough to be my grandfather," Mill said in between his laughter.

"I've heard some talk about you, Raheem," Floyd said and continued. "You're still growing too. The word is you should tighten up a little on your defense and rebounding. Most scouts see you growing into the three position with your wide shoulders and your height. Before it's over you'll probably be six-eight and around 250," the wise old ball player told the young Raheem.

Then he went on, "How about your SAT scores?" The group began to assemble themselves into the steamy old gymnasium while this conversation continued.

"I take them this coming year," Raheem said, now perky because of the questions about academics.

"Have you been studying?"

"Yeah, I just need to sharpen up on my calculus, everything else is good. I love reading and I have good comprehension and essay writing also."

The much older Floyd patted the larger by several inches--and growing by the second–Raheem on his back as if to say, "You'll be alright, kid."

The two sides did a very brief shoot around and stretching warm up before they quickly started the rough house pick-up game.

Raheem took off toward the basket off the in-bound to Bo from Malik. Bo lobbed the ball to Raheem after a brief dribble across half court for the dunk. The exact same play Bo and Raheem did to all unsuspecting opponents at the start of every game. They were batting 1000 on that play and each time the two executed it, Bo got more enjoyment than the last. Raheem simply got back on "D" without saying one word. He was remembering what the old veteran had just told him about commitment to rebounding and defense.

Floyd took the point for his team of vets. The old head team's game of play was very similar to what Raheem had seen when they had played the college squad a few weeks past with one exception.

"Get down low, Prince," Floyd said as he dumped the ball down in on the center for an easy two. "That's all day Prince," Floyd said as the old heads ran back up court.

Bo made a quick adjustment. "Double down on Prince, and on offense we can run him to death." This was a good plan in theory but in practical application it proved to be much harder to execute by the younger players. Raheem and Bo did their usual run and gun style of undisciplined play where Floyd and his band of over 30s banged the paint out with each trip back in transition.

Raheem had made a conscientious effort at playing excellent defense and it was manifesting itself on the court. He had several steals on a very quick and intelligent player with a legendary street ball resume by the name of Willie Mack. Mack found the teenager extremely hard to cross over or out-run. When Raheem was on offense, he blew past Mack on isolation at the top of the key. This happened on two consecutive plays. When it appeared as though Raheem would drive to the basket for a dunk, the old heads collapsed the middle attempting to give the youngan a hard foul. But before they had completed the attack from both sides, Raheem faked a driving lay-up with his right hand, pulled the ball back and around his back to his left hand, and passed the ball to his approaching bag man Mill down the right baseline for the dunk. That's a wrap!

"What schools are you leaning toward," Floyd asked Raheem as the two chatted in front of the recreation center.

"I don't know, if Reem was alive I would probably be going to Georgetown with him, but now I just don't know," Raheem said with a slight grimace at the thought of his deceased cousin.

"You ate lunch? Come on and take a ride with me," Floyd offered.

"Yo Bo, I'm a ride with Floyd," Raheem yelled across Fourth Street to Bo as he got in his car.

"Arr ight, hit me later; we might team up with Floyd and them so learn somethin while you ride wit um," Bo chided.

The two drove to a southern-style restaurant in the center of the city called Momma's *Soft Touch*. Momma's was known for having excellent food, professionally cooked with huge portions at an affordable price.

"I ain't got much bread, Floyd," Raheem said.

"You don't need no money when you riding with me youngan," Floyd said without looking at his young student. The two entered the quaint restaurant still dressed in their gym clothes with towels wrapped around their necks. They were immediately met by a lovely, well-built brown-skinned sister dressed in a flowing sun dress that accentuated her thick backside.

"Good afternoon, guys, will it be just you two?" The young lady was trying not to stare at the shoulders on Raheem.

"Yes, just us," Floyd said.

"Follow me, please.

Floyd tapped Raheem on the arm three times to make sure he wasn't missing the afternoon matinee. The two had a seat on opposite sides of the booth and picked up the waiting menus.

"I know what I want," Floyd said as the host walked away. "But I think that she'd rather have you, youngan," Floyd chuckled.

"I'm cool, I want some fried chicken breast and buttermilk waffles!" Raheem clearly was much more interested in eating lunch.

"Yeah, I'll have the same."

When the waitress came the two ordered and then continued with their basketball talk.

"Have you heard from Temple?" Floyd was talking to Raheem but his eyes were on the backside of the waitress as she walked from their table towards the kitchen.

"Like almost every week, I want out of Philly, though. I want to see what it's like to be out on my own," Raheem replied.

"How about North Carolina," Floyd quizzed.

"I got a letter from them a while back but I haven't scheduled a visit yet."

"If you want, I could handle that for you. I could also set you up on a good AAU team at the end of our league play on 16th Street." Floyd then continued, "I got friends in New York who wanted you at the 2 slash 3 spot. Today you played big. I'm thinking you'll end up a small forward before long."

Raheem was listening but the delicious tasting chicken breast mixed with the sweet syrupy buttermilk waffles had his growing body on cloud nine at the moment.

"I'm gonna get your left hand in order this summer too," Floyd said in between bites.

"This summer?" Raheem asked with a mouth full of the golden brown spicy fried chicken.

"Yeah, I spoke to your boy Bo about us all balling together this summer. In the meantime, how would you feel about me helping you out on a few fundamentals? Not too much needs work, but your left hand could get better and I'd like to see you develop a low-post maneuver."

"Yeah, what you got in mind?" Raheem sat back from his plate for a second.

"I gotta figure on you growing at least a few more inches and, with your shoulders, you will put on much more muscle in time. At some point down the road you might play the four position."

"Yeah?" Raheem had always enjoyed playing the guard positions with his speed and smooth stroke. The four was for slow brutes he'd always thought.

"I know what you're thinking, but the four has really changed. Soon the four will be like an extra guard because of all these seven foot white boys that are coming over from Europe. They got game man. They don't play like Frankenstein no more. Their footwork is excellent and all of them can shoot the three ball."

"I been noticing that in the NBA."

"Yeah well, your game had better evolve too if you want to stand out among the big boys some day. Never rest on your laurels youngan; always work to get better."

Raheem shook his head up and down in complete agreement.

The two wrapped things up at the table. Floyd paid the tab and left a hefty tip for the waitress. As they ventured toward the exit, the young hostess called to Raheem, "Excuse me..."

"Who me?" Raheem was surprised and was pointing toward himself.

"Yeah, you big man," she replied flirtingly with a welcoming smile.

"What's up," Raheem now smiling too.

"My name is Juanita, what' yours?"

"I'm Raheem." He had clearly gone through this routine a million times.

"Oh, you too cool to holler at me?" Now the young woman was showing some attitude.

"Naw, I'm good, my phone is in the car so take my number," Raheem said with the confidence of an old player. As the two exchanged numbers with the promise of a future date, Floyd watched from his late model BMW 6 series with envy. "Man, what I wouldn't give for one more shot at being young and four or five inches in height," the old vet thought as Raheem's huge shoulders turned toward the care and he took long smooth strides before opening the door to get in.

It was then that Floyd had made a decision that he, and only he, would manage Raheem's career and his future in basketball; he just hadn't expressed this decision to Raheem as of yet...

Chapter 5

"What's going on?" Raheem questioned his next door neighbor as he walked toward his steps with his head twisted around to his left looking across the street at all the police activity in the cemetery.

"They found a body a few hours ago," the young Puerto Rican female neighbor told Raheem as she stood half way outside of her screen door.

"Anybody say who it was?" Raheem asked slightly interested but fairly numb to bodies being found in the cemetery.

"Some young girl who was out there like that. Polo said she O.D.'d. The old head who was banging with her ran when she went out. Then three other fiends stole all her stuff while she was lying on the ground. Polo bust one of the fiends up side his head and made him call the wagon and report her death."

"Oyeah, good for him," Raheem said with a half smirk while shaking his head up and down with approval as he went up the steps into his house.

"Nana said make sure you clean that back up and walk Gonzo; he ain't been out of that back yard in three days and it stink!" Kia was speaking of the small cement patio behind their little brick row house. It was hardly a "back yard."

"Shut up!" Raheem barked as he pushed past his little sister.

"Come here boy!" Raheem yelled to the large pit bull that had started to run all over the house with excitement. "Come here, I said." The dog cowering, now lay on his side with his tail still wildly slapping on the floor as Raheem latched his chained leash to his collar. Raheem and Gonzo left the house and started down the street. Just after rounding the corner and walking down a second block, a group of young men with several pit bulls of their own were upon them.

"Unleash him, Yo, let's see what he cut like," said a small member of the group, with a dark complexion and wearing all red plus a fitted hat sitting backwards on his head. His own pit was snarling and at the end of the leash pulling on his pint-sized owner. One of the other young men (who was also dressed in mostly red) said, "Just let him go."

"Naw, man, my dog aint' no fighter, he's a house dog," Raheem said and began to try to walk away. The words weren't out of his mouth when the other owner let his leash go and the ensuing fight began. The two dogs went at it ferociously. Gonzo was so strong and his head was so big that he had his opponent on his back within seconds. Gonzo may not have been trained to fight but the fight was in him. After it became apparent that Gonzo had a death lock on the little gangster's dog, the young man began to submit.

"Get him off, Yo, make him break."

"Let go Gonzo, let go boy," Raheem, as large as he was, now struggled trying to pull Gonzo off of the other pit bull. Finally after what seemed like at least several minutes, Gonzo broke as if he had been fighting for years.

"Yo, my dogs fucked up, man, look at his neck. Plus he acting funny." The pit bull was having trouble breathing and it appeared that his trachea could be crushed. The dog was in real trouble. The other young men were getting upset also. "He's gonna die, man," one of them cried out. On cue the dog laid his head on the cement sidewalk.

"Yo, you killed my dog, Yo," the small gangster was really upset and looking at one of his friends just before giving him the cue to shoot Raheem.

"Him or the dog, Little Knowledge?" questioned the taller boy with a nine millimeter now showing.

"Both, shoot him and the fuckin dog," Little Knowledge yelled.

Just as the boy pulled his gun completely out from his waist, Tito's worker, June, pulled up to the group in his low rider. From the driver's side window *POP POP;* with the two quick shots he hit the boy in his hip and in his right hand where the gun was resting. June pulled his car up on the sidewalk, and shot at the running group of gangbangers hitting Little Knowledge in his ass.

"Aw man, he shot me in the ass, Ima die."

"Shut the fuck up you little bitch," June yelled. "Cmon Raheem, get in."

"Ima die, I got shot in my ass, Yo, I'm hit in the ass," Little Knowledge kept yelling as the two sped off and headed toward Ninth Street to tell Tito what had happened.

Tito took all this in stride. "Don't worry bout it, June, just tell everybody to be on alert," Tito was telling June while Raheem looked on not knowing what to say.

"Damn, June, I don't know what to say, if you hadn't of come pullin up I might be dead."

"Don't worry bout that, just stay clear for a while till we cool this shit out between these gangbangers." June was only 16 himself but he had at least eight years on the street as a hustler and two as shift commander. He was very comfortable in his position and clearly had no problem shooting people.

As Raheem lay down in his basement bedroom he had his hands folded behind his head, feet crossed looking up at the ceiling. He thought to himself how close he had once more come to meeting death. Raheem wondered to himself how there could be so much death and destruction at every turn. Then he took himself to his safe place, deep in the back of his mind. He was on the court dribbling with his left hand. His father, or a figure that he had come to call his father, was on the court coaching him on.

"Put your right hand behind your back and lay up with your left. Come on, run back, dribble with your left only. That's it son, great job man!" The man always complimented Raheem in his day dream as well as during his sleep. Raheem always ended up being taken to a barber shop with his father and out for a quick bite to eat.

"So Dad," Raheem called him. "What will the Lakers do now for a big man?" His father always spoke with deep wisdom and with a clear and complete understanding of all and every conversation. He was the perfect Dad.

"The Lakers will always come up on a great big man sooner or later," the figure responded.

"Yeah Dad, you're right, they always do." The two got the same haircuts, and ordered the same meal off of the menu.

"How are you feeling about the ACC?"

"I kind of like the Big East, Dad; what do you think about Villanova?"

"Nova! Great school son. We have to work on your studying for the SAT's," said the larger figure whose voice had now become omnipresent in Raheem's mind. And as peacefully as Raheem's dream had been, violence invaded in an instant. Kareem was dribbling up court the wrong way.

"Why are you dribbling backwards, Reem?" and as Raheem followed his cousin and tried to get him to respond, Kareem's eyes turned black and his chest exploded splashing dark blood in Raheem's face. He struggled to catch his breath in the wetness. Sucking for air, Raheem opened his eyes to a wet tongue from Gonzo.

"Gonzo, get the fuck off me!" Raheem yelled at the dog. "Who let Gonzo down here?"

"You gonna start walking him twice a day and wash him at least twice a month," Mother Porter yelled down the steps from the kitchen. "He's your responsibility, baby," Mother Porter continued as she did her morning chores starting with a huge breakfast and several loads of laundry.

Raheem rushed to get dressed in shorts and tee-shirt. Quickly he took Gonzo across the street to the cemetery to handle his business. Raheem was sure not to unleash his dog certain that Gonzo would bite one of the sick dope fiends who were meandering in the cemetery for a free shot from one of the whores who had tricked enough money to get a sunrise score. Gonzo sniffed around in a circle then started his business about fifty yards deep into the once beautiful park-like pet cemetery that, many years ago, was the final resting place for the pets of the wealthy upper crust of North Philadelphia. Raheem looked just beyond his squatting dog and spotted a man fixing his arm with a black belt. A rail thin white woman with dirty matted hair and black fingernails was in the bushes with her pants around her calves. She had track marks all around her entire vaginal region.

"Hurry up bitch," the impatient man said while the woman shot up in her pussy. Raheem looked unmoved. He had been living within close proximity of the filth of drug use his entire young life. This was nothing he hadn't seen many times before.

"You done, boy?" Gonzo growled and snapped and he wiped his hind feet on the thick grass. When Raheem turned, a young twenty-something Black girl was behind him. She was thick and healthy looking but that didn't fool Raheem.

"Can I drain that thing for you young boy, I only need a five spot to get a bag of Dead Calm."

"Naw, I'm cool," Raheem said as he began to walk Gonzo out of the filthy den of a shooting gallery that was once such a beautiful place...

Chapter 6

The air was warm and balmy. The music was loud and full of bass. "Cash Money" was blaring. Cars lined the avenue on both sides. Hot Dog and Pizza trucks were lined up on 16th Street and ice cream and water ice trucks were lined down 15th Street. The young females were wearing very little in an attempt to advertise all of their assets, all adorned with hair and nails looking perfect. They paraded in hopes of being seen by a traveling baller. It didn't matter what type. Football pro, basketball pro, drug dealer, player, paper boys AKA check & credit card scammers, anyone willing to spend time and money on these show girls. The local radio station, Power 99, was present as well as several local celebrities. This was opening night of Philadelphia's Summer League Basketball Play. A must-see event for the who's who in the street life. Philadelphia's living legends of street ball were all present: "Sad Eye" Jackson and his squad, Blair "Silk" Floyd with Bo and Raheem's crew, Kevin "Hook Head" Evans with Chester Ringo and "Bad Foot" Wood, and lastly "Young Lito in his Prime" Anderson headed the list of Philly's best ballers and must see. You could feel the energy in the air. "Big Scratch" from Gratz Street was the sponsor for Young Lito's crew and they looked awesome.

Blair Floyd had gotten wind of this event and all the festivities that were planned well beforehand and got a booster from North Carolina

University–who wanted Raheem to sign–to give him $25,000 for the start of the summer. He was given orders to spend as much as possible directly on Raheem. The last summer payment was to be spent on a car of Raheem's choice.

"Lakers uniforms!" Raheem said with glee, as he dug through the boxes in the white box truck a block away from the hallowed courts. "I hate the Lakers," Bo added, clearly not moved by Floyd's choice.

"We got new runs too," Raheem saw the colorful sneakers stacked in the back of the truck.

"We get new runs every week for the summer and two warm-ups and game suits," Floyd said in a very business-like tone. "Our sponsor will also allot $200 per game for each of you. But for you college boys, you didn't ever receive a dime. Got that!" Floyd looked directly at Bo. "Especially you high schoolers. We wouldn't want to ruin your life in college sports before you even get out of high school."

"Got it Floyd!" All agreed in unison. The other players were less enthusiastic. They were, after all, adults with real jobs or they were hustlers. A few hundred bucks a week and new sneakers with bright colors weren't going to make or break them. This was about redemption. They had lived past their prime basketball years and no pro team had called. Street ball was all they had left. As for Floyd, this was his vehicle to keep rich boosters handling over fat envelopes with wads of fresh one-hundred dollar bills. This was Floyd's livelihood.

Each year that passed, Floyd had a new crop of high school ballers that he directed to the school of his choice. For a growing talent like Raheem, he could get close to a quarter million dollars. Not including host money for Raheem's grandmother and her expenses. The other young boys on Raheem's crew would be much easier to get but not nearly the same amount of cash. Floyd moved smoothly in big basketball circles. He was well known throughout the ACC, Big East and the Atlantic 10. His name, Silk, wasn't just for his smooth play but for his silky smooth demeanor. He was the direct line between rich white college boosters or even fanatic fans of particular large universities who just happened to have great amounts of disposable income to lavish upon the families of young basketball players to be lured to their beloved schools. After all, you are unlikely to find a white businessman paling around the syringe ridden basketball courts of the "Badlands." Floyd in all of his legendary demeanor was more than happy to take on such a task for the proper fee.

Tip-off for the first day of play showcased the "Sad Eyes" team versus a team out of Bucks County for game one of the night. It was, as expected a highlight reel for "Sad Eyes" and an eventual blow out. Sad Eyes had recruited his sister's son from the west coast for the event. Marquis Jackson was headed to UCLA. He and his uncle provided plenty of excitement for the crowd. Long threes, high flying two-handed shots behind the back and dunks. Alley-oops snatched from mid-air and under the leg dunks. Amazing cross-overs and knock downs–where a player dribbles so well into his cross-over that the defender over reacts and falls to the ground from the fake-out. None of this stuff was exactly fundamental basketball and, in fact, most college coaches would bench a player for such acts. But for the street baller, these moves are all directed toward pleasing the crowds. When a defender hits the ground or is even staggered, the crowd goes wild. And don't let the offender make the shot after such a move, the crowd goes into a frenzy. This is the life of street ball.

The next game was "Young Lito in his Prime" and crew versus Kevin "Hook Head" Evans and "Bad Foot" Wood and crew. It proved to be a much more conventional game. "Young Lito" was a hard pounding point guard with a deadly three pointer. He and "Bad Foot" went at it all night. Shot for shot. In the end, "Hook Head" and "Bad Foot's" team were simply too big down in the paint. Although Lito had dropped 33 on them, "Chester Ringo" made three clutch three-pointers at the end of play. It proved to be a very successful opening night for the Summer League Play.

Raheem's team would not play until Thursday night but Floyd handed out white envelopes anyway.

"What's this?" Raheem asked as he put down his fresh new gym bag that was adorned with the words "Badlands Lakers" in purple and gold and contained all of his fresh new gear.

"It's what it is," Floyd said as Raheem counted his money. His envelope contained $500. He whispered to Floyd, "I think I got too much."

"You didn't get enough, boy. Just make sure you keep your mouth shut," Floyd said like a stern old head and not a team mate. The rest of Raheem's crew were just as happy about their good fortune.

Night one of ten was in the books and as all the ballers prepared to go their separate ways it became rumored that there would be an after party at the Hilton in center city. Big Scratch and Young Lito pulled up back to back in black and white 5.6 Mercedes Benzes.

"What's up, Floyd?" Young Lito called out of his window.

"What's happening, Lito," Floyd responded as he shook hands with his old friend. "This is Raheem Porter," Floyd offering Raheem over to meet Lito.

"Yeah, Kareem's Lil Bra, right? I hear good things, young buck. North Carolina is it?" Lito said as he stepped out of the car.

"Yeah, maybe," Raheem towering over the short older baller as he shook his hand.

"That's a good fit for you. I'm sorry to hear about your Bra, man. He was a real good dude and a hellava baller."

"Yo, Shorty, I don't' know bout you but I got traps to check and bitches to fuck," Big Scratch yelled from the big black Benny.

"Thanks, Lito, I appreciate that," Raheem said.

"If you need anything, any help at all, give me a call and I got you," Lito said as he got into the large vehicle that looked as though it just rolled off of the showroom floor with every inch of chrome shining.

"Man, them boys is up!" Raheem said to Floyd as he hopped into his BMW 7 series. "I mean, you up too, Floyd, but damn!"

"Man, that shit don't mean nothing, plus them boys still throwing stones at a penitentiary wall. You can't go to prison for what we do. All we do is ball, period! Nothing more, got me?" Floyd was yelling now.

"Yeah, I got it Floyd."

"Now you are gonna need a tutor for your SATs; I got that taken care of. Here is the number," Floyd said as he handed Raheem a card. "She is gonna pick you up and drop you off. No fuckin around, learn that shit."

"What's up with the hotel party?" Raheem asked with a smile.

"Not for you, Homie, not yet. You'll have your turn. Hotel parties aint' no place for a 16 year-old to be. Plus, I promised your Grandma that I'd get you home," Floyd said as the two pulled up to the beginning entryway of the Badlands at Germantown Avenue and Somerset Street.

"It always amazes me how once you pass this point it's open season. I got to get yall out from around here," Floyd said at the sight of all of the dope fiends walking around and the out of town tags that carried the white kids from both New Jersey and Delaware for Philly's high quality heroin.

"It ain't so bad Floyd, once you get used to it," Raheem said in an honest tone.

"Sheeit, I ain't never gone get used to it. I hope you ain't sneakin and fuckin none of these night walkers. I don't care how fat the ass, she might have that ninja!" Floyd spoke as he looked at a pretty brown-skinned girl in tights trying to stop the car. "I know it's real tempting, but you have got to be strong." Floyd's voice tapered off as he watched her ample backside giggle when she turned to show the goods.

The two pulled up to the Porter house and Floyd offered a few more proverbs. Raheem was a good student. He absorbed all that he could from his new-found mentor. He had surmised that most of what Floyd had been telling him was in his best interests. Somehow, Bo did not always see it that way. Bo was already committed to the University of Cincinnati and therefore was of little use to Floyd outside of summer league play. The rest of Raheem's crew were watching closely to see what, if any, benefit Floyd would bestow upon Raheem before they put all their eggs in his basket.

"Tomorrow you have a big day Youngan, so get some sleep," Floyd said.

As Raheem walked up toward the front door of his row house, Kia's voice rang out. "Don't even come in, Nana said go walk Gonzo!" Kia handed him the leash with Gonzo on the end pulling as usual...

Chapter 7

"My place is right here, apartment two," the shapely dark-skinned tutor said as she placed her keys into the keyhole of the apartment door. Raheem was surveying the place as he often did out of habit. He noticed how the apartment building hallway had several bicycles leaning here and there but none were locked. There was a large UPS package up against the wall next to another apartment. Even a few plants neatly sitting inside of decorative ceramic pots at every few doors.

"Let me turn up the air first. Hoo! Please take your shoes off and leave them at the door," the sexy tutor said as she fiddled with the thermostat.

"You live alone?" Raheem asked as he looked over the place. He was fixated on the photos on a table in the living room that connected to the dining room and the small galley kitchen. The pictures appeared to have been taken somewhere outside of the U.S.

"Yes I do. Oh, I'm sorry, just me and Mr. Popples," she said as her large black cat purred for attention.

"Where are these pictures from?" Raheem asked as he still looked over the entire décor of the place which was an eclectic style of collections from anywhere and everywhere that the young professional had traveled.

It was a mish-mash of stuff but all organized in such a stylish way, one that Raheem was not used to.

"Those were taken in Paris, France," was the quick answer as she stood in front of him with her hair now out of its wrap and her hands backwards on her lower back just above her protruding supple buttocks. She was clad in form-fitting yoga wear. The young Raheem could smell her perfume. Not the cheap stuff that his sisters wore. This was some "French shit" he thought to himself as he tried to be cool and was pushing himself to appear very adult-like with his questions and tone.

"Okay, Raheem, first we'll hit math. Today we'll start with Bayes Theorem and conditional probabilities. Then I'll have you read things and write a short essay on what you've read. That will give me an idea where we are at concerning your reading comprehension." The sexy tutor spoke as she unfolded a portable whiteboard and got the work set up. Meanwhile, Raheem was trying to get his young mind right. He had watched her behind so long that he now had an erection. It was utterly impossible to hide, given his size, and the loose gym pants and tee shirt seemed to just accentuate the problem. After the tutor finished her set-up and turned, she first noticed the sheepish look on the young Raheem's face. At first she couldn't figure out what was the problem. She thought to herself, maybe the young boy farted and is now embarrassed. And finally she saw him trying to hide his huge erection with his long arms.

"Okay listen, we have two hours a couple times a week until you take the test. My job is to ensure that you do well enough to get into all the top D-1 schools. I'm paid very well for that. I get a lot of referrals for the great work that I do. So what do we need to do to have your full attention? I'm not letting you fuck me, so forget that. You're 16 or 17 or whatever you are."

Raheem now was totally embarrassed because of having caused such a conversation. It showed all over his face. "I'm, I'm sorry Ms, Ms..."

"Call me joy, Raheem; I told you my name three times. I guess it's my fault anyway. I know how you young boys are." Joy's voice was trailing off as she exited the room. She reappeared with a lotion bottle and a box of tissues. Without so much as a word, Joy got in between Raheem's large legs. She reached for the pants inseam strings and untied the sweats. Then, taking both hands she reached around and helped Raheem pull the sweats down to his ankles. His erect penis was standing at full attention clearly a microcosm of its owner who now stood just over six and-a-half feet tall. And he was only into the summer of his junior year with lots of time left for another growth spurt.

Very business-like, Joy squirted the lotion on her hand. Raheem could smell the perfume more pronounced now than he had smelled on Joy earlier. Joy wrapped her small soft hand around the head of his penis, then taking her right hand and doing the same with its shaft. Very methodically she stroked up to the tip of the head and down to its base. She stroked the head once or twice more seeing a jerky reaction from Raheem's body and kept her concentration there on its fleshy portion. When Raheem opened his eyes and saw Joy's face and her pouty lips were agape in what seemed to be deep concentration; he blasted off like a NASA rocket headed toward the moon. Joy stroked faster and harder to ensure that the young boy would be completely empty and satisfied enough to pay attention to her lessons. Joy cleaned Raheem up like a new born baby having his diaper changed. Then she gently pulled his pants up. She took all the soiled toiletries off to a waste basket in the kitchen and washed her hands. After re-entering the room she simply stated, "Shall we begin?"

Show Time

Thursday night it was show time. Raheem, Bo, Mill, Moop, Malik, Floyd, Prince, Willie Mack and Ben Mitchell were all in game mode. They were playing a team put together by a pill and codeine dealer named Juice who was from 17th and Jefferson. The headliner on the team was Jerome Biggs. The brother of a Philly NBA legend named Pooh Bear Richards. Juice had all the best that his money could buy. He was upset that Sad Eyes had chosen to play with another team. It didn't matter at this point. Juice and all parties involved surmised that Jerome could make anyone around him look like a star with his Jason Kid-like point guard skills. Plus he had not one, but two seven-footers, both were bums but seven foot nonetheless.

The tip-off was won by Mill over "Lurch" number one. Jerome's slow big team was unaware of Bo's famous play and soon fell victim. Mill to Bo and then Bo lobs to Raheem after the take-off. Raheem had to bring the ball up for the dunk because of Bo's missed lob. It actually made the dunk look just that much more fantastic. He caught it flying past the basket and had to reach back with his left hand for the spectacular dunk. The crowd went wild! Sonny Hill was with Power 99 on the side and quoted that Raheem was higher than he had seen anyone in summer league play going back to Doc in the 1970s.

Raheem blocked it all out and focused on the next transition when the slick Floyd stole the ball from Lurch #2 and flew his 40 year old legs down court. But instead of a simple lay-up, years of play and instinct told him that he had a trailer. That trailer just happened to be his young protégé Raheem. Floyd threw the ball off of the backboard hard, a flying Raheem caught it with his left hand and arm fully extended almost making a backwards "C" for a ferocious Lebron James-like dunk. For the entire game, Raheem continued to perform like this. It didn't matter who guarded him, it didn't matter if he came from his left or his right. Jump shot, after jump shot, passes, blocks, rebounds, but most spectacular were his dunks. They were absolutely magnificent. All night long he dunked with either hand with clear and equal ferocity. It was a masterpiece performance.

The following morning, while he stuffed his face with her usual huge breakfast, Mother Porter handed her grandson the daily newspaper. In the sports section was a very clear picture of the young teen. He was flying through the air in a statuesque-like pose. The *Philadelphia Daily News* sportswriter was raving about Raheem:

> *"In a town looking for the next great sports star, they need not look too far from home. A young teenager by the name of Raheem Porter took several street ball legends to school last night. The triple double alone won't do justice to the performance of epic proportions produced by a boy not yet 17 years of age. It was as if the great 19th century impressionist Claude Monet himself had created this God-like figure, appearing to almost pose in midair. Sure it may be a bit too soon to crown the next best baller but I'd be damned if I didn't see the best performance that I've seen in 25 years."*

"Thanks Nana," Raheem simply said, not reading too much into the article. He knew that too much coverage would alienate his teammates, especially Bo. So instead of exuberance, he felt a bit anxious waiting first to hear from the fellas. Just then his phone rang. "Yo," Raheem answered.

"Did you see the paper?" It was an excited Bo yelling on the other end of the phone.

"Yeah, I saw it," Raheem now very relieved that his friend was okay with the article.

"What's up, what you got going today?" Bo said.

"I got this SAT tutor stuff to do, real hard stuff to learn."

"Yeah, well, if I could do well enough to get into most schools then I'm sure you can"

"I hope so; this calculus is a mug!"

"Yeah it is, but you just need to learn enough to pass the test, not master the work. You got me? It's all multiple choice man, pick an answer and move on. It's just like making a decision on a split-second pass. You read the defense and feel where to pass the ball."

"Damn Bo, that makes so much sense man. It's like Floyd said too; when you put in the work, why worry. Because you know that you have prepared.

"Floyd said that, huh?" the air over the phone had suddenly gone bad.

"Yeah, well you have said it in the past to me and Reem too." Raheem was making an effort to keep things smooth. The young Raheem clearly understood just how fragile Bo's ego was, especially since he was no longer the best baller in the crew. For years he was and he was Kareem's older friend with advanced skills. Bo was still the older–by two years–friend, but his athletic and ball skills were no longer comparable to the ever-growing Raheem. In fact, with Raheem on the court Bo simply disappeared.

After Raheem completed his telephone conversation with his friend he finished off another full pack of bacon along with a half dozen eggs cooked over easy. He then made a brief trip to the back yard to clean up some trash and dog poop. Finally, he then headed upstairs for a quick shower. He dressed in his new gear that was purchased with the $500 given to him after his last game. Raheem had handed over last night's money to his grandmother. When he gave her the money, her initial response was a cautious one. "Raheem, Momma don't want you in those streets, I don't care how much you make, you hear me!" But Raheem explained that this money was from the sponsor and he was certain that Floyd had told Mother Porter. In the end she told Raheem that, "I need to talk to that Floyd again."

Beep, Beep, Joy's horn to her small Honda sounded. Raheem splashed on some Michael Jordan cologne, put his fitted Phillies cap on backwards and was out the door.

"Come here!" Mother Porter yelled. Raheem instinctively ran back and kissed his small, authoritarian Grandmother on the cheek and hugged her. "Always be a good boy, you hear me Raheem" Mother Porter said this almost tearfully as she let her only grandson go. "I will Nana," Raheem said as he ran out the door.

"Hi Joy," Raheem said once settled into the compact car with the seat back as far as possible.

"Hello Mr. Raheem. Did you sleep well? We have plenty of work today and I need to review last week's work." Joy was talking continuously in between sips of her mocha latte. Raheem was thinking about her dark smooth unblemished skin. Her French manicured nails and her jet black shinny hair. She always smelled like lavender and now he could see her muscular legs because of her tennis outfit and bobby socks along with her cute pink and blue sneakers to match.

Joy wasn't like the girls from the Badlands. She was clean of both drugs—all drugs, not even weed or Xanex, which most all the girls did one or the other, and tattoos. "Maybe she had one on her ass," Raheem thought. "Awe Man, her ass! Just like a perfect bubble." Raheem had jerked off twenty times to the thought of her ass. He must have made too much noise in one of his private fantasies because Mother Porter had yelled, "What the hell is going on down there, boy. I know you ain't got no girls down in that room Raheem." Now here he was, once again face to face with this twenty-four year old grown woman. His youth began to manifest itself even before the two exited the car. Joy, still having a one sided conversation, continued to talk. As the two entered the hallway of her Old City section apartment an older white female neighbor was closing her mailbox and preparing to exit.

"Hi, Joy," the woman said.

"Good-morning Ms Landenburger," Joy responded. As Raheem politely held the door open for the elderly woman he had totally forgotten about his erection. The woman looked at his pants and looked up at him and signed in disgust. Being much shorter than the 6' 6" Raheem, she was just face-to-crotch and clearly felt violated as she squeezed by.

"My word! Young people have no shame," Ms Landenburger said as she began to walk down the two steps and toward the park. Raheem fumbled to fix his pants but it was of no use. No matter what he did, it still looked very bad. Following Joy into her apartment, Raheem's erection was pointing directly at her ass. She turned to say, "Take off..." but changed her words in mid-sentence to, "Here we go again; you're like a little horn dog humping the air." Joy then said, "Come on, let's get this over with so we can study." The two walked toward her bedroom and Joy started to lecture the boy.

"At least you ain't all disrespectful with it. If you were older, Raheem, I would be inclined to see where this could lead, but you just so damn young." Raheem was totally entranced by the sexy Joy. His eyes were fixated on her sexy walk, her cleanliness and her proper speech. He wanted Joy. He wanted Joy more than anything that he'd ever wanted in his young life. He wanted Joy almost as much as he wanted to meet and be friends with his father.

"Sit down on my bed." Raheem now robotically complied. "No, go to the head and lay back." Raheem was as high as a fiend on pure heroin. He closed his eyes and just as if he were in his basement bedroom with his hand clasped behind his head, he drifted off. Joy was totally nude. Silky smooth and dark–perfectly dark like Swiss chocolate. He could smell her scent even before she had opened herself up to him. Joy spoke soft and confidently.

"I'm gonna do me this time Raheem," as she struggled to climb to the top of Raheem's peak. "You just be a good boy, Raheem, always be a good boy." As Joy had now fixed herself into a good riding position, facing him with her French manicured nails now digging into Raheem's chest. The gangly boy watched her perfect breasts bounce back and forth in rhythm with her riding motion. She was moaning loudly and for the first time, Joy was no longer in control of herself. Back and forth, back and forth. She took in all of Raheem's penis and yelled in ecstasy. "Come on, cum Raheem, come on my love." As Raheem began to release himself inside of her, he opened his eyes.

"Com on man, you was taking too long."

Raheem was half way completed when he realized that Joy was still stroking his penis with both hands. "Ahhh ahhh," Raheem yelled now because he was super sensitive to her touch.

"Man, this tutoring gig is becoming hard work dealing with you, boy," Joy said as she cleaned Raheem up. Then they walked toward the hallway bathroom. "Get yourself together boy, you're running late."

"Ah man," Raheem quietly said to himself as he noticed that Joy was not nude but fully dressed.

Chapter 8

The days had been flying by and the matchup between the undefeated team of Sad Eyes and Company versus the Badland Lakers was coming in near. Each team played the other twice. Therefore, even with a loss or two, the chances of still making the finals continued to be a very real possibility.

Raheem and Floyd hadn't played on the floor at the same time very often over the last few games. Floyd wanted to watch Raheem's game from the sideline as often as possible. Even though Floyd had one of his assistants video all of the games as well as the team practice, there was nothing better than real time observation. Floyd explained it this way: "It's like being at the Hershey Park arena and seeing Wilt the Stilt scoring 100 points or simply seeing clips of it for the last 50 years." He had all of Raheem's games, practices, and even a few of Raheem's breakfasts and lunches recorded. Floyd was a smart man. He had been around the game his entire life. He knew from experience that he held the golden goose and he was prepared to monitor Raheem's every move. Some day in the future, all of the hours of video on Raheem would be worth a fortune.

"Kentucky is here tonight," Floyd quietly informed Raheem.

"Oh yeah?"

"Yeah, and so is Duke."

"Duke?" Raheem said this with a bit more excitement.

"Duke ain't for us Heem."

"I always liked Duke, but they never contacted me."

"Yeah, well I'll explain it to you later tonight, my feelings about that," the wise old head told Raheem as they stretched out before the game.

"Yo Heem, I just saw a guy talkin to Mister Sonny, they say he's from Duke," Moop was almost shouting toward Raheem with his excitement. And then he added, "Yeah, so you had better play some defense then."

"I always play good D."

"Not from where I'm watching...I'm just saying, maybe you play good D when I'm not around." Moop was just needling his good friend.

"Yo, did..." Mill was cut off in mid-sentence by Moop and Raheem, "Yeah, we heard already."

After tip-off Raheem had made an effort to play more team ball. His usual sprint to the basket wasn't finished with his patented flare of a thunderous dunk. Instead, opting to dump the pass off to the trailer, Malik, for the easy layup and foul.

"Smart play," Floyd yelled. Bo, however, did not particularly like the play. Bo and Raheem had been doing that same play for five years, all the way back to when Raheem was still under six feet tall and unable to dunk.

Raheem had immediately made an impact on defense. He had two blocks on the switch down in the paint and one of the blocks was on the six foot-ten inch Georgetown center who was playing for a group of guys out of West Philly. Those guys were sponsored by Will Smith by way of his old neighborhood friend and former body guard, Charlie Mack. The team was tight. They ran the court well with Bo and Raheem in transition. They played man-on-man defense and switched to double Raheem if he tried to drive. Floyd had called a time out when things looked too tight just before half-time.

"Raheem, you play the one, Bo, go to the two, Mill, you're out, Willie Mack, you're in. Shoot they lights out. Three guard set...Ready, BADLANDS!" The new set-up was perfect. Raheem was very comfortable passing the rock. His dribble with either hand was just as good. On the inbound, Raheem took his team on a fast break trip. Once at the top of the key, he dumped off to Mill down low, Mill passed up high back out to Willie Mack who quickly hot potatoed it to Raheem. Heem took off on the baseline but faked a layup and passed back to Willie Mack for the three. This went on all night. Raheem easily achieved his fourth triple double, however, the grumbling crowd of the street ball watchers wasn't impressed. A high flying act in the summer league is a must-see.

"Save the fundamentals for college," one young man shouted out. But, as far as the young ladies were concerned, it didn't matter what Raheem did. "Raheem, I love you," one girl yelled. "He is so fine, I want to have his baby," was a voice that came from another group of girls sitting a bit closer to his bench.

The game had been a tight one but the young bucks from the Badlands had once again prevailed. "Great game, Raheem, you are really maturing," the sports writer for the *Daily News* said to Raheem.

"Then how come the college people from Kentucky and Duke aren't talking to me?" Raheem sounded perplexed as he questioned Floyd.

"NCAA rules, they aren't permitted to talk to you like this. In fact, you don't see them wearing Wildcats gear, do you? That's because they are not on school time. The same with Duke."

"Well, how did you know where they were from?" Raheem, still looked a little confused.

"Everybody knows, and now you know too."

Raheem hitched a ride home with Bo. Floyd was meeting with two men from Kentucky. Floyd and the two recruiters who had absolutely no official title with the actual university met at Philadelphia's infamous Melrose Diner. "Isn't this the place where the mob had a few hits in both the 80s and the 1990s," said the middle-aged dark haired guy. He was over six feet tall, looked like an older former ball player who had remained in good shape.

"Yeah, I told you about this place," said the shorter of the two men. They sat down and looked over the menu. "I'll have the meatloaf special," said the short man. "I'll have the T-bone with potatoes and some ice tea, please," said the taller one. The waitress looked like she'd been waiting on tables for many years at this place. She scribbled down both men's orders without making eye contact. "And you, sir," she addressed Floyd while still looking down at her pad with her pen poised to write.

"I'll have a bowl of oatmeal with bananas and a cup of coffee," Floyd responded without looking at the menu. He kept staring at the middle-aged waitress and the way in which she'd smeared a slash of red rouge across her cheekbones. It looked more like war paint and he wondered whether she realized how clownish she appeared.

"Talk to us Floyd, what's the haps, as you guys like to say," the smaller man said as the waitress walked away.

"The haps, as you say, is this. Bo is already signed and committed to Cincy, Moop is headed up the street to St. Joe's and Mill and Malik are up in the air." Floyd dug into his bag and pulled up some stats sheets on all of his young prospects.

"Let's just cut to the chase here," the taller man from Kentucky said. Why didn't we know about this Raheem Porter?"

"You did know about Raheem." Floyd was playing his trump card well.

"I got a sheet on that kid that looks absolutely nothing like what I've heard or what I saw tonight."

"Yeah, well, that's what happens once I get hold of a growing talent. Plus he grew about five inches since I first spotted his cousin Kareem."

"Yeah, sad thing there. He was a possible for us too," one of the recruiters said as the waitress returned with their food. After she brought their drinks, the men resumed their conversation.

"We want him, Floyd; he'll be good for the great Commonwealth of Kentucky and by God, it's our Christian duty to see to it that he gets there. Can you understand us Floyd?"

"Floyd speaks in tongues too, and right now the Holy Ghost is telling me that there are big numbers involved, especially since God was speaking to someone else down on Tobacco Row." Floyd was beginning to expose a small portion of the "cards in his hand."

"Ah, those good ole boys with horns, they have absolutely no authority or influence over that little self-righteous point guard. Really, tonight they were simply watching a game." Clearly the older business-like man was assuming that Duke had made a pitch for Raheem. Only Floyd knew how far off the men were. When making reference to the little point guard, they were speaking of Duke's head coach and his past as a guard for West Point. In between bites of steak, the negotiating continued.

"Well, that may be true about them, but there are several plantations down there on Tobacco Row and more than one has a need for good niggas and I got the best buck available, bar none." Floyd looked up from his empty bowl of oatmeal, wiped his mouth with the paper towel to the right of his bowl. There was silence at the table. Floyd picked up his hot cup of coffee. "Black, I love it like this."

The negotiator sitting directly across from Floyd was beginning to turn red. "Give me a price you fucking nigger," he quietly said with clenched teeth.

"Ah, the good Christians have exited the building. Well I just happen to have an answer for that too." Floyd, once again, dug into his bag and passed two sheets of paper to each man. The sheets of paper looked like itemized accounting statements with a listing of services rendered by three different companies. The payments amounted to one million dollars. Conveniently, nowhere on the sheets was a mention of Raheem Porter, Blair Floyd or the University of Kentucky. Simply business that had nothing to do with basketball.

"This is doable."

"Not so fast," Floyd said. "This is what I want in cash." The next number was simply written by Floyd on the coffee-stained paper towel. It was an extra $150,000.

"What, you greedy bastard!" The one man said quietly but the woman at the next booth had heard him and turned to look at who was arguing.

"It's money well-spent, guys. I'll give you Raheem for at least two years. You do good business, I'll keep Kentucky on the reverse negro migration plan. I don't care what it takes. If the baller is in my region, I'll get him there." Floyd spoke with a strong air of confidence. He was now in complete control of the meeting. "You got one week to think it over, and the fee rises 10 percent after that. Push comes to shove and I'll go up the road."

Up the road, of course, meant the University of Louisville. And the two men knew Floyd so they knew that he wasn't messing around. Floyd had missed the boat in playing for an NBA team and his retaliation for not being taken by a major university in the late 1970s which would have given him a platform to be seen by pro scouts before the media boom was to control who went where in Philadelphia and the surrounding tri-state area. In some cases, Floyd had heavy influence on the future for ballers as far as New York and west to Pittsburgh. Smooth as silk. The young ballers loved him. He was, after all, a street ball Philadelphia legend and still in good shape to run with the best of them. That not only gave him credibility, but it also gave him respect from the up-and-coming best.

So, as Floyd walked out of the infamous Melrose Diner, it was as if it were the 1980s mob wars all over again. Only the two warring factions weren't Italian and their weapons weren't guns. Floyd hopped into his late model BMW with the confidence of a Fortune 500 CEO, fully aware that his hugely inflated bonus would get paid...

"What's the deal with you and Floyd, man?" Bo asked in disgust as they stood leaning on his SUV directly in front of the Porter home. Several male fiends were speed walking past them and counting one dollar bills as he asked the question.

"Yall got something new," one of the dope fiends asked.

"Man, get the fuck out of here," Bo shouted at the men stinking in filthy clothes. Feeling no shame or disrespect, the group of young men went on their way in search of their next fix.

"I mean, what's with the one-on-one? He always pullin you up. He drive you home. I know you got all that gear cuss of him."

"Bo, I never questioned you about your truck or your spending money. You even bought me two pairs of Jordans at the end of the school year, so why you hatin on Floyd?" Raheem said this sadly because he and his good friend were at odds over something that was such a well-known practice.

"I ain't hatin on him, I'm just sayin. You like a brother to me and I need to know what's goin on with you, Heem." Bo was saying this as two girls were now walking past them pulling on a blunt of weed.

"When have I not told you what's up with me?" Raheem said pleadingly. The teenaged girls dressed in mini-skirts then stopped a few feet away to display themselves to the fine looking young men.

"Yeah, well I told you that I wanted us to play together at Cincy, Heem. But, Floyd hates Cincy."

"He don't hate Cincy, it's just not for me, that's all," Raheem said with a less than convincing tone.

"What's up, Raheem, you don't see us," one of the petite light-skinned girls protested.

"Yeah, I see yall, hi Shayla, hi Abby."

"Hi Raheem, they both said in unison."

"Let me and my brother finish rappin and we'll get at yall, awight?" With that, the two girls walked up 9th Street to make busy until Raheem was ready for them.

"How can you say Cincy don't fit? I'm your point guard, Heem." Bo protested and continued, "You come out next year, by then the team could belong to me and you. We could convince Mill and Malik to come with us. Man, I'm trying to win a college chip and head on to the pros. Shit, all five of us should make it."

"One step at a time, Bo, let me get out of high school first and get through these SATs," Raheem spoke with the maturity of a young man much older than his 16 years of age.

"Yeah, you're..." Bo was interrupted in mid-sentence by a loud and rapid "boom, boom, boom, Kplow, Kplow!!" The unmistakable sound of a Russian made Kalashnikov AK 47 echoed through the block. Both Bo and Raheem hit the deck. Instinctively, they both got flat down on the ground. Bo crawled under the front end of his truck while Raheem lay flat on his right cheek with his arms spread out. He was giving it his best effort to get as flat as he possibly could. "Kplow, Kplow, Kplow, Kplow," rapid fire continued. "Boom, boom, boom, the sounds of an American made large caliber handgun was responding. Both Bo and Raheem could hear the patter of running feet and men yelling. "Mira eti, Mira alli," followed by boom, boom boom. "Mira, mira alli," bloom bloom, and more running feet. It seems that young gangbangers in red had made a move on Tito's men. Both Polo and June lay in the middle of the street. Raheem could see Polo's face between the cars. His eyes were open and looking directly at Raheem. Raheem knew that blank look. It was the look of death. June was also hit but Raheem couldn't see his face nor could he see movement. He only heard the words spoken in Spanish, "Look over there, look over there."

Several men had exited homes on 9th Street with fully automatic weapons and began shooting at the five or six youth who, in their confusion, tried to run through the cemetery toward Germantown Avenue. They figured that they would be safe once across "the line" and fully into the Black community run by an old gang called the Mighties. Tito had a great deal of respect for the Mighties and wouldn't want to hit a neighbor who was neither a gangbanger or a drug dealer. The young men, not being very smart concerning warfare, didn't do their due diligence; if they had, they would have known that Tito kept several shooters in the park and they would have run the opposite direction. Each teen shooter was quickly gunned down in the park. Then, an older man who had come out of one of the houses walked over to each of the youth lying on the ground and, standing overhead of their lifeless bodies, methodically shot each one in the head until their faces and heads no longer existed. All that was left was a bloody mess of unidentifiable pulp.

Chapter 9

Blair Floyd was very comfortable in his Rittenhouse Square condo on the 34th floor. From the vantage point off of a small balcony just outside of his living room, one could see from river to river. Floyd lived in one of the newer buildings surrounding the old brownstones in the Rittenhouse section of Philadelphia's most unassuming wealthy residents. He had previously been denied residence at the more prestigious Rittenhouse Square Hotel Building which was actually a co-op so ownership had to first be approved by a board and then voted by a co-op group of owners. The Rittenhouse Square Hotel building was old and distinguished like most of its occupants, and their rules were just as old and distinguished. He never stood a chance of buying into that place.

So, when a new condo building went up for the first time in 40 years, it became grand news. At first, Floyd thought that he would be priced out of the bidding for one of the luxury units during the housing boom of the early 2000's. But, lady luck would smile on Floyd as she would frown towards the original owners. The real estate bubble burst and all existing development projects were beginning to see red ink. Before the decline and recession Rittenhouse Square could have easily received an average price of five million for a 2500 square foot two-bedroom apartment. The developers were overextended and they got greedy, asking as much as 10 million for a three bedroom penthouse with parking. They were so certain that the units would be completely filled as they were building it, that the developers foolishly overleveraged their loans by almost 40 million dollars. Once the recession hit its stride, along with the collapse of the subprime lending mortgage market, banks were calling in all major debts. The rookie developers had gone from feast to famine in just over a year-and-a-half.

This economic shift left 80 percent of the brand new units in the most prestigious part of Philadelphia unoccupied. The foreclosure was swift. An auction was held for the who's-who of big real estate. In no time flat the project was up and running again. Floyd's realtor phoned him with the welcoming news.

"Floyd, these people are practically giving these condos away. I can get you a two bedroom for $800 thousand." Floyd, being the savvy businessman, understood that the market was near rock bottom. If he played his cards right, he could have a gem on his hands once the market rose up from its ashes.

"I'll tell you what, reserve us a one bedroom, two bedroom and a three bedroom. Negotiate the best deal for all three units."

"But Floyd, how do I wing the financing?" The realtor sounded doubtful that Floyd was possible of carrying out such a deal.

"You let Silk handle that," Floyd sounded very confident.

The realtor was able to negotiate a great deal because the units weren't moving as well as the auction house would have hoped. In the end, Floyd was able to secure three condos facing the historic park and square for just under $2.5 million. Not only did he get the financing, but he got it via wire transfer the same day that the contracts were signed. Additionally, Floyd made the owners of the building agree to his terms on apartment layout and sign an agreement stating that he could never be forced out by any owner's group action.

Two years later, Floyd sold the one bedroom that faced the park for almost $2 million. He had almost recouped his original investment for all three units. He was leasing his two bedroom unit to one of his own companies and writing it off as a tax deduction. The truth was he was using that space as a clothing closet and as an apartment for his two voluptuous Dominican maids. At last check, the condo was worth close to $3.5 million.

One floor up is where Floyd lived in a three bedroom 3,500 square foot luxury suite which was simply immaculate. Floyd had truly learned to do it big and he did it bigger on the backs of young ballers and the boosters who just had to see their schools recruit the top players and win, win, win. Money to them was simply of no great importance; just a means to an end. Floyd understood this and that's why each year he worked his tail off gaining the trust of at least three or four top prospects in the country. At up to $500,000 a recruit and well over one million for a player of Raheem's caliber, adding that to his consulting firm for several mid-level and big schools, plus his growing real estate empire, Blair "Silk" Floyd was doing pretty got damn good for himself.

Floyd was just getting comfortable with a foot massage from one of his Dominican maids dressed in only a sports bra and small panties. The smooth sounds of the great John Coltrane were softly playing throughout the hidden speakers strategically scattered all throughout the condo. The lights were dimmed down to a warm low glow.

Floyd sipped his long-aged XO cognac and reveled in the moment. He was a long way from his days in the Richard Allen Housing Projects. With his "bo bos" sneakers purchased for $1.99 from a huge basket in the center of the supermarket's "no frills" section. No, that Floyd no longer existed. Silk had "arrived." He was now rubbing elbows with Philadelphia's distinguished elite. On his coffee table that held his snifter and his Monte Cristo was a golden envelope. Inside was an invitation to a $5,000 a plate fund raiser for both the sitting Mayor and a U.S. Senator. He was invited simply by his address alone. Just for that reason, Floyd would attend. He was also in constant thought about the safety of his golden goose Raheem. "I have to move on them," he thought to himself.

"Popi, te recesito como nunca henecesitado un hombre," the beautiful cleaning woman at his feet said. She could have been speaking Russian, Floyd didn't understand one bit of Spanish. Just as long as the women were at his beck and call and didn't violate his trust in any way. That language was international. "Do like Popi say, do like Popi say." And everything went smooth. One major slip-up and Floyd would be learning Chinese at night instead of Spanish...

Chapter 10

It wasn't long before the same detectives who had investigated the murder of Kareem-and done a half-assed job of it–were now investigating the gangland style shootout and murders of Polo and the gangbangers in red. June had somehow, through the grace of God, survived. Raheem's little cousin Kia had been at his bedside at every opportunity. Mother Porter really liked June and was upset that he'd been shot but she was quite apprehensive about Kia's constant bedside vigil.

"Them shooters could come right in that hospital and try to finish the job," Mother protested when Kia would beg to go see her heated crush. Kia had been saving her money that Mother Porter was giving her from all her work in the kitchen. She had $500. All she needed was for June to say the word and she would secretly brand herself with a fly tattoo adoring his name. On her lower back maybe or even on her ever-growing teenaged tight ass. Mother would never find out. The word would first have to come from her June. Kia had never given herself to any boy; June would be her first and only. She had secretly told her girlfriend next door about her virgin status and that she would welcome June as her first, but she'd never tell her cousins. "Shit, Keema's hot ass would do it to him just to spite me," Kia had told Lisa next door.

"What's up?" June quietly whispered the words.

"Hi June," Kia stood up once she saw that he was awake. "How you feeling?" Kia sounded genuinely concerned.

"I'm fucked up. They took out my spleen."

"What's your spleen?"

"I don't know, I just know I aint' got one now."

"I tried to bring you white potato pie but you ain't allowed to eat," Kia said sadly.

"Yeah, it's gonna be a few days they said."

"There was a bunch of girls here but your Mom said that I was your sister so the nurse let me in."

"Where is my Mom?"

"She went back to her house to check on your little brother. I can't stay long; my Grandmom don't like this stuff. All this gun stuff and killin."

"Yeah, I know, I can feel her," June said with an understanding tone.

"June, is you gone stop playin the corner now?" Kia had tears in her eyes.

"Naw, that's my job, Kia."

"Yeah, but you the corner shift boss ain't you? Why you gotta be out front all like that?"

"You right, I guess. I gotta get outta here first, then see what Tito say." June was pressing the button for the nurse believing that it was a morphine drip. "This shit don't even work. I'm still in pain." Just then, the nurse came in the room.

"Yes Little Mister," the Jamaican woman said.

"I'm in pain and this drip ain't working Miss," June struggle to get the words out.

"Alright tin, me be right back wit your shot. Time to leave little lady. Sister, huh," the nurse said as she exited the room.

"I'll be back tomorrow, okay June?"

"Yeah, thanks." Kia gingerly leaned over June and gave him a light peck on his dry lips. She looked at her teenage love interest with both sadness as well as sheer hope in her young heart...

"Yes mam, I do understand. I assure you that I have Raheem's, as well as your entire household's, best interests at heart," Floyd said in response to Mother Porter's concerns about Raheem's safety as well as his nighttime activities.

"What really concerns me is all this money, Mr. Floyd. Raheem gave me $500 the other night and he tried to give me a thousand two nights ago. Now what kind of basketball playin a boy 16 years old doin to make that kind of money," Mother Porter spoke as she folded her arms and looked Floyd directly in his eyes. She stood there waiting for an answer. Floyd took a long, slow sip of the strong hot coffee that she had prepared. Then he cut a small piece of the white potato pie that she had given him as a guest in her home. He placed the fork, loaded with the pie, into his mouth, slightly closed his eyes and savored the taste. "Um, very good." Mother Porter hardly blinked an eye and simply waited patiently.

"Okay ah, Ms Porter," Floyd began. "I'm gonna give you a crash course in economics. And either you and I are gonna have a mutual respect for each other, and you and this entire household will be moving shortly to a house of your choosing, or you're not going to see eye to eye with me and in a few years Raheem will be standing out there on 9th and Indiana playing gun tag with a bunch of crumb snatchers. If you're lucky he gets his own package and makes it big. He buys you a house and five years later the Feds come a calling and not only take Raheem, they take your new house. If you're unlucky, well, we already know what happens in the Badlands when a family is unlucky."

"Talk to Momma about this economics," Mother Porter said, now sitting up at the table with eyes that appeared to soften.

"There's a good way of doing things concerning young athletes bound for college and then there's the right way of doing things. The question here is which one suits this family. The good way is, you have a man like myself who acts as a buffer or a shield between the boy and the family. The college knows nothing about this arrangement, ever! There are people who would love to have your grandson play at a particular school. These men are business men. Totally legit men. They are willing to take care of the family to lure the child to whichever school they choose. However, there can never be mention of your boy and these men in the same breath. That's my job. You never know who these people are and they don't know you."

"Can we go to prison for this?" Mother Porter was listening intently and was showing her concerns.

"No. However, if it can be proven, Raheem would be barred from playing college sports because he would be deemed as a pro athlete." Floyd continued, "Do we follow each other this far?"

"Yes we do," Mother was sharp and clear.

"Okay, now we have the right way of doing things. You accept no financial help at all. You operate on hope. We hope and pray that it all works out. The NCAA and colleges accept Raheem and in five, after he plays for some school, he might go pro and by God, it all works out. Well, I believe that God helps those who help themselves. The NCAA rules are good for white kids with wealthy parents. For us from the Badlands, what are we left with? You gone sell enough pies to get Raheem through four years of college, clothes, TV, sneakers, food and books? He's gonna need a little car. Then what about the girls? I respect your hustle Mother Porter but let your grandson help you out. You give me the word and I'll walk the bride right up to the pulpit." Floyd now stared at her.

"What kind of money are we talking here and what about my Grandson?"

"I can guarantee a house within a month. You tell me where."

"Yeah, what about money," Mother folded her arms defensively once more.

"At least one hundred, maybe more."

"One hundred thousand?" Mother Porter's eyes were wide open as she dropped her arms to her sides.

"Yes", Floyd said, "And of course, Raheem's car or truck will have to be in your name." Floyd continued, "All of Raheem's expenses will be taken care of."

"And how do I possibly explain all of this good fortune?" Mother Porter was sharp.

"Good question, but we will handle all of that through trust with some attorneys."

"What about Raheem, where does my baby go?" Mother Porter sounded like she was at the end of her questions now.

"Another good question. We are in talks with a few boosters. Right now it's between North Carolina and Kentucky but you never know. If you are on board, we can start your house hunt immediately. The sooner the better. Better to buy a house before Raheem signs a letter of intent." Finally, Floyd closed off with his lecture. "Here is the good faith money." He passed Mother Porter the bulky brown envelope that had been sitting beside him on the table. He then stood up and slowly offered his right hand. "As the Jewish businessmen would do it." A deal on a handshake, all we have is our word." They shook, and with that, Floyd turned and exited the Porter household. "Kiss Grandmom goodbye, Raheem, we got a game to play."

Chapter 11

Mother Porter took the manila envelope that Floyd had left. She tucked it and its bulky contents under her arm and exited the kitchen. "Hi Nana," Kia said as she came into the open screen door.

"Do your Nana a favor and tidy up the few coffee cups and pie plates in the kitchen. I'm a little tired I'm going up stairs early."

"Okay Nana," Kia said cheerfully as she closed the door to their small home and locked clicked the deadbolt lock. Mother Porter entered her bedroom and shut the door behind her. She slid the small bolt lock on the door shut to provide some assurance of privacy. Sitting on the edge of her large bed that seemed to engulf the entire room, she pulled the envelope out from under her arm. The envelope was clasped shut as well as glued so Mother Porter reached to her old armoire and pulled out a letter opener. She slowly and neatly opened the envelope, reached in and retrieved three stacks of fresh $100 dollar bills with a brown paper wrapper around each one printed with "$10,000." It was a total of thirty thousand dollars. Mother Porter's heartbeat picked up just a bit. Although she'd been saving for years at the bank and had close to that amount in her savings account, this stack of cash in her lap gave her a very different feeling. It took Floyd 30 minutes of conversation to hand over 30 thousand. It had taken Mother Porter 30 years to do the same.

As par-for-the-course, the night was alive. The music was jumping. It was as if the real "Show Time" of the 1980s was in town. The Summer League was growing with each night. It had become the place to be. There were more foreign and domestic late model luxury cars lining the surrounding blocks than at F. C. Kerbeck's car dealership in New Jersey. The women available at the games were numbering almost 7-1 and that wasn't the good looking women. Add them and those percentages went up. One writer from a hip hop magazine wrote that "...there was so much pussy available that you could open a cat store." Yep, the Philadelphia Street Ball Summer League was having its turn. The entire basketball nation was finally watching.

"I need you to play your game tonight. Look at me!" Floyd snapped at Raheem. "This is your stage tonight. I know you don't like to do it, but I want you to put on a little bit of a show. Right hand left hand, two-hand, double pump, Jordan sideways, long threes just do absolutely you!"

"Alright Floyd, I'll give it my best shot," a humbled Raheem said as he thought about the possibility of his own father being in the crowd of all those people who filled the stands and lined the gates outside of the courts. He day-dreamed of what his Dad might say to him right now as he prepared to go up against a legend like Sad Eyes and his nephew.

"Go right at them, son. You're bigger, stronger and faster. Plus you think the game throughout. Pass quickly and then move without the ball each time after you pass."

"Yes Dad," Raheem quietly mouthed to the figure in his head.

The tip-off went to Sad Eyes' team and since they were just as quick they completed an outlet pass for the wing man headed toward the basket. Raheem, having done this to others a thousand times was mentally prepared once he saw his team had lost the tip. Instead of waiting, he was already back on "D" preparing for a break by either Sad Eyes or his fleet-footed nephew. The quick no-look pass took place and was immediately picked off by Raheem's long arms. Both Bo and Floyd were out in transition from their three guard set. Raheem completed the long pass to the old vet who bounced-passed behind his back with his right hand to a speeding Bo for a flying one-handed dunk that began just inside of the foul line-it was like watching Julius Erving back in 1976. The packed crowd on the outdoor bleachers as well as everyone on the fences and those in the windows of the surrounding Temple University apartments went wild! The opening statement by "The Badland Lakers" was clear. "We are here to win." Sad Eyes was not the slightest bit moved. His years of experience in street ball as well as most of those years at being the very best of the Summer League, gave the man an air of confidence that most top level NBA pros only wish that they could possess. He had his well-trained and talented nephew at the helm pushing the rock. Sad Eyes was always best with the ball in his hand, but those were his younger days. He had now taken a later Michael Jordan approach toward the game of being an on court manager with a deadly fade-away jump shot from absolutely anywhere on the court. "Ain't no place safe," Sad Eyes yelled at Raheem as he continued his assault!

Sad Eyes from the left baseline; Swish. Sad Eyes from the top of the key; Swish. Fake by Say Eyes, drive down the middle behind the back finish finger roll with his left and the foul! Sad Eyes was single-handedly killing the Badland Lakers at the half. The score was 58-42 and Sad Eyes had 25 points to himself.

"I'm out," Floyd said. "We are gonna run all young boys. Yall just do you. Run the court from out the gate. Let's check Sad's legs."

At the beginning of the second half, Raheem got a pass while free-running under the basket and dunked Kobe-style on the way by. He then turned to press the ball on the in-bound. The pressure was tight and nephew gave up the ball to Malick who lost the ball in haste but Raheem scooped it up and reversed dunked once more with extreme ease. Again the press, but this time Sad's team passed out of it. Once in half-court set, it became Sad Eyes versus Raheem. The crowd came to its feet, Sad Eyes took the challenge but just as he began his patented crossover dribble, the quick hands of the teenage superman picked his pocket like a Center City criminal and looked like he had been shot out of a rocket as he sped up court.

Without thinking, Raheem launched from the foul line with the ball in his right hand and at his waist. Seeing that it was now impossible to make the dunk with his right, he turned sideways. Jordan-like, he leaned into a dunk with his left! Absolute pandemonium erupted! The court had to be cleared of the crowd. "You got that on film, right! You got that on film?" Floyd yelled to one of the four videographers that he had strategically spaced on each corner of the court to film Raheem's each and every move.

"Time the fuck out," an uncharacteristically emotional Sad Eyes shouted. Over on the opposite end of the court, Floyd, the great General Silk, was just that--*Silky smooth.*

"Two minutes gang and don't let up. Keep your tunnel vision. Now is the time where legends are made. Rappers are gonna be rappin bout this shit in years to come. Badlands on three; one, two, three, Band Lands!"

The next two minutes were just as if Floyd had scripted it himself. The thousands who looked on watched in utter amazement as Raheem appeared to float on air for several fantastic dunks that were unlike anything that have ever been seen before. One sportswriter who was on the sidelines said, "It was as if Greek mythology had reopened its ancient books to add one more god–the flying Raheem." It almost appeared as if he could defy gravity for as long as he saw fit. Another ESPN sportscaster reported to his audience that, "The freakish contortions of his torso in mid-air would make a seasoned yogi jealous." Simply put, this was a performance that all athletes and common folk alike had never seen and most likely would never witness again–unless young Raheem saw fit to bless them once more.

"Can I talk to you, Floyd?" A white middle-aged man who Floyd knew from his past dealings was from the state of Kansas. Floyd, you got a minute?" Another older white guy and his wife probably from Michigan were also vying for Floyd's attention at the same moment.

Raheem's price had just gone up. In fact, as he and Floyd packed up, Floyd had mentally doubled the price and he suspected that it could triple after he got a look at that video. Some college or university would make millions from Raheem simply wearing their uniform in a year from now. As for now, Floyd's job was to protect his golden goose.

"Floyd, who are these people?" Raheem wondered to his mentor. "Just get your stuff and we're out," Floyd barked back as he took a few of his business cards out of his pocket and then he and Raheem quickly jumped into Floyd's spanking shiny new Range Rover. "Man Floyd, this is nice," Raheem said as he looked around at all the fresh calf skin leather and wooden veneer that trimmed the inside of the brand new vehicle. "Do you have a driver's license?" Floyd asked the young Raheem.

"Naw, not yet," was the reply.

"Well, we just have to take care of that." While Floyd was still speaking, his cell was vibrating off the charts. "Yes, how may I help you?"

"Mr. Silk," the man on the other end said sarcastically.

"What's up," Floyd was realizing that it was the boosters out of the Blue Grass State.

"Do we have a deal or shall I say, we are prepared to make a deal," the voice on the other end sounded a bit urgent.

"Well, I'm no longer sure that we are in negotiations. Things have a way of changing when you take too long," Floyd replied while smiling a big grin because he fully understood what was at stake.

"We're on I-95 North right now with a gift for you."

"It ain't my birthday man, why give me a gift," Floyd replied dryly. "Listen man, give me a call in the morning around 10 a.m." And with that, Floyd hung up the phone.

Chapter 12

The following week was handled meticulously by Floyd and his entire team for Raheem. He had perfectly scheduled each hour of Raheem's days. The life of a teenager in the big city can be deadly but for a Black teen to gauge the danger properly, you would probably have to compare it to the same percentages of a Marine on recon or an Army grunt serving in war-time Baghdad. Floyd understood this challenge better than most. He had lost more than one top prospect to the street violence that plagued the African-American community. With this in mind, Floyd was working around the clock to relocate Raheem's family as soon as possible. Raheem loved the Badlands but as his legend grew, jealously was sure to begin to cause the young man a great deal of trouble. It was the trade-off for greatness in a not-so-great neighborhood.

In his downtown Center City Philadelphia office, Floyd and his staff were hard at work. They had found the perfect prep school for Raheem to complete his senior year. They had also found three choices for Mother Porter to choose as her new home. Two were in Montgomery County which was home to upper middle class whites as well as the business elite depending upon which township one resided. Kennett Square was in neighboring Chester County–nothing to do with Chester, Pennsylvania which is in Delaware County. In the end, this was the place Floyd had picked for the family. It was a tightly knit enclave with both working class and wealthy.

Floyd's staff had found an Italian style home on four acres for just over a million. He was now asking three million for Raheem's services for a mere two years before he would exit for the NBA draft. Of course, that didn't include the bag money. Floyd loved bag money. The cash always helped recruit the next family or persuade a tough acting father or uncle who somehow believed that they could do a much better job of managing their young prospect than he could. Cash always had a way of softening up the hardest of parent or sibling.

"You have the Kansas husband and wife business team waiting in your office, don't be long, because some people from a tech company need to talk to you. They flew in from Palo Alto, California. I think it's Cal State's people." The sexy white assistant whispered the last part of the sentence to Floyd who was all business, dressed in Armani with a Bill Blass shirt and olive green lamb-skin shoes. Floyd was tall and dapper. His haircut was impeccable, an inch-and-a-half all the way around. The lines on his shape up were as sharp as a razor. His waves flowed like the Atlantic and were plentiful like sand on the beach. Floyd took a quick look at his Patek Philippe with the diamond bezel and began toward his office. As he entered the room, the 50 something husband and wife team stood to greet him.

"No, no, please be seated," Floyd very politely shook the husband's hand firmly and looked him in the eyes. The very elegant tan-skinned wife stood as tall as Floyd and her long flowing golden locks gave Floyd a huge smile that brightened the entire room.

"We've heard a lot about you Silk," the wife said.

"I hope I'm not as bad as I'm made out to be Mrs. Kozlow." Floyd was at his glass bar pouring short tumblers of single malt scotch.

"I'll have a vodka and soda with lemon, and please call me Jill." She nodded toward Floyd.

In a country drawl, Floyd went on, "How can I help you fine folks from Kansas? Tom is it?" Floyd handed Jill her glass and then Tom.

"Well, it's like this," Tom said and then took a sip. "Ah, that's good there." He closed his eyes after a taste and then continued. "I heard about that boy all the way in Kansas but seeing what I saw last week, it don't do justice to talk about him. We are a part of a very unique group of business people. Our media business is deeply tied up into college sports, particularly, the University of Kansas. The money that football and basketball revenues generate in our communities is off the charts. Simply put, we need boys like that to sustain our bottom line. We are not representing the school in any way. Let me repeat; we have no ties directly to the school in any official capacity. That being said, I am here with my checkbook or I can wire 3.5 million to your company as an investor along with a letter of intent that you'll handle with the boy."

Floyd was looking cool and collected as he sat behind his big dark wooden desk with celebrity photos of him with all the past and present ballers. Both street legends, like his friend Sad Eyes, and New York City's Pee Wee Kirkland and NBA greats like Magic, Larry and Dr. J. Yes, Blair Floyd was as smooth as silk.

"What are your thoughts...ah...ah...Mr. Floyd," Tom now looking just a bit uneasy.

"Well my thoughts are pretty straightforward. Three and a half mill is a little low, don't you think? This kid has NBA great written all over him. I have half of Silicon Valley waiting to give me California. Not to mention them slave traders down on Tobacco Row. Their racist asses are beating the door down. Did I mention the Blue Grass State? Well, we all know what kind of money them horse trainers and breeders got down there."

"So, what did you have in mind Floyd?"

****

Raheem had passed his driver's test with flying colors. His big bright smile on the license said "Under 21" Raheem Porter. He couldn't stop looking at it and smiling. This had not gone unnoticed by the assistant who had accompanied him.

"Would you like to drive us home, Raheem?"

"Hell yeah, this is a Benzo." Raheem quickly got in on the driver's side.

"Raheem, I thought that you were a gentleman?"

"Oyeah, I'm sorry, I gotta get used to this stuff." Raheem ran back around the rear of the Mercedes C class and opened the door for the 20-something beautiful office assistant. She was petite, with a short haircut and very fair skin. Although Raheem favored very dark-skinned women, Tammy was so pretty with her hazel eyes and her tight little body he almost swore off of his fantasy with Joy to focus on Tammy.

"Just get all of your mirrors in place before you put it in drive." Tammy was patient and warm. Raheem wanted to do everything correctly. He felt a need to impress her in every way. He reached for the radio and Tammy lightly slapped his hand. "You need uninterrupted practice and that means no radio."

"Aw-ight, aw-ight," Raheem shook his head in agreement with the lovely Tammy and quite easily compiled.

"Where to?" Raheem asked with a big smile.

"Well, at two o'clock we are supposed to meet your family at your new house to see if your Grandmother likes it. You haven't had lunch yet and neither have I.... soooo"

"Yeah, lunch sounds great to me; lunch always sounds good. Say it slow, luuuunch."

"Boy, you are crazy Raheem," Tammy said with a bit of a cute giggle. Then she continued, "Okay then, what would you like for lunch?"

Clearly Raheem was thinking "her" but figured that would be definitely a bit too vulgar to say to such a classy girl like Tammy. "I want chicken or turkey and salad. Floyd said that I wasn't eating properly so he has a dietician writing out my eating schedule and diet. My Grandmother don't like it. She says a man should eat like a man. The dietician has far too many vegetables and fruit and not enough red meat. All kinds of fish, protein shakes and oatmeal. Plus, I'm supposed to eat seven times a day. Chicken and turkey twice a day. It's just too much to remember," Raheem said as he shook his head in disgust.

"Yeah, well you'll be grateful down the road as you perform better and better. Diet is key to an athlete's performance over the long run."

"I thought that's what practice was for," Raheem was simply being a wise ass as he flashed a big grin towards Tammy.

"You know what I mean, boy," Tammy had once again tapped Raheem on the arm playfully. It seemed like a definite signal to each of them that the two had very good chemistry...

Chapter 13

"Didn't I tell you to stay in this Mother-fucking corner! Floyd yelled over the classic sounds of Miles Davis. He was dripping with sweat, standing completely nude. At his side in his right hand was a short black leather whip with approximately ten tentacles. With each spoken work he whipped the wealthy businessman, Tom Kozlow, who was squatted down in the corner completely nude with both hands tied behind his back. To add to the humiliation there was a red ball strapped firmly into his open mouth; he couldn't make any significant sound, just a bit of a groan. Floyd had been whipping the powerful businessman for up to three long songs now. Mr. Kozlow had finally passed out from the pain and shortness of oxygen. Floyd looked at the weak and beaten business tycoon and then at Mrs. Jill Kozlow as he lay with his face down and his ass up in the air. Floyd's erection was full and hugely grotesque. Mrs. Kozlow had been enormously excited thus far but with the thought of Floyd taking her husband, she was overcome with ecstasy. She was totally nude and beads of sweat dripped from her forehead and then down over her ample breasts. Her excitement was exposed by the love juice dripping from her crotch and running like a small stream down over her thighs. She had yet to be touched by Blair. Floyd dropped the whip and bent down to Mr. Kozlow's face. He removed the strap and the red ball then checked his breathing. Mrs. Kozlow sighed in disappointment that Floyd had limitations.

"What do you think, I'm some type of barbarian?" Floyd just glanced at Mrs. Kozlow but clearly the question was merely a rhetorical one. He slowly walked toward the bed and reached for Mrs. Kozlow, tugging at her long blond hair. With a his firm left arm he flipped her over to expose her evenly tanned round ass. She quivered under Floyd's dominance

"Time for me to invade Kansas," Floyd said as he began to enter her aggressively from behind. He fucked her methodically, like a machine and continued to whip her husband all night long in his Rittenhouse Square Condo. The following morning they had a deal. The couple was so completely satisfied that not only had they agreed to all the financial demands from Floyd but they also approved hundreds of hours of free use for one of their corporate jets. Floyd would be written in as a business investment. He would now be able to fly throughout the country in search of top shelf athletes on the behalf of the Kozlow's business–which was college sports. By no means was Floyd willing to be a slave to Kansas and the Kozlows.

"Our company owns the TV rights to the University sports Floyd. Just give us a jewel each year. There's only one Raheem, we understand that, but keep us in play and a few million a year plus perks is very easy for us to do. Mrs. Kozlow was closely watching Floyd at breakfast. She drank her orange juice and strolled back toward the master suite. Mr. Kozlow took note of his wife walking toward the suite and turned to Floyd.

"I need to make some calls, Floyd, and tie up the few loose ends to wire this money to the accounts given. Would you be kind enough and entertain Mrs. Kozlow for a while?"

Floyd didn't like being told what to do; he didn't even like it when he was told to do something that wasn't his idea first. But, the Kozlow's were so far ahead of him that they had flown in with a half million in cash. So, why not play their game?

****

Business was sporadic on 9th and Indiana since the shootout between Tito's workers and the young gangbangers. The Homicide Division had enormous pressure placed on them because of the special that the USA Today ran on the Badlands. The high quality of heroin teamed with the rising homicide rate made the Badlands appear to be a lawless land akin to something from the movie *Mad Max*. People were dying of overdoses or being shot on a daily basis. The entire area for blocks was patrolled by sick drug addicts and out of town vehicles in search for the best bag of dope each morning. Prostitution was a 24-7 activity that kept the streets littered with women who were very likely sick with HIV or full-blown AIDS from using shared and dirty needles.

The truth was that 9th Street wasn't the only corner in the Badlands nor did it always have the purest dope. What 9th Street and Tito did have that most corners lacked was sheer meticulous organization. Polo was dead, June was in the hospital and the heat was on. For almost any owner of a major drug corner this could have resulted in the sounds of a death knell. Not for Tito, 9th Street was his. It didn't belong to the City, it didn't belong to the neighbors or the Jewish owners of the homes that most of the Blacks and Puerto Ricans rented, and now even with the mobile Police Trailer and the constant vigilance by the Homicide Unit, Tito was determined to keep his running flow.

During the day he had workers scattered throughout the small alley-way behind Mother Porter's house and her neighbors. The fiends were directed through several different homes throughout the day. They would go in, but never come out. They exited the back of the house into the alley to purchase and into the back of a house that was facing Mother Porter's house and neighbors. The fiend would then exit that house out the front and onto 8th Street. So while the cops watched 9th Street, the fiends were leaving from 8th Street...

Although the Porter household was doing much better, old hustles were hard to break. Mother Porter was now selling twice as many platters out of the back door. On this day, however, she had stopped long enough to view the new house. Floyd had a car pick the family up to take a ride out to Chester County and check out where they were going to be moving. The ride out to Kennett Square was like a ride to the moon in some ways. As soon as the family started to drive through Fairmount Park the lush green of grass and trees filled their senses. Then the driver headed down Route 1 towards their new home. As they approached Kennett Square the quaintness of the village seemed like something out of a movie. Main Street in this town had some antique shops, a few restaurants, and not one but two brew pubs. Everything seemed so clean compared to the litter and filth that was ever-present in the Badlands.

The drive took them through the village of Kennett Square and about a mile-and-a-half down the road was an entrance with a freshly paved driveway. As they turned right into the driveway there was no house immediately visible, just a long row of trees flanking the driveway. Finally, the house came into view. The house wasn't over the top, it seemed to fit perfectly with the surrounding landscape. Mother Porter took a deep breath when she first saw the house. It was beautiful and the plantings around the house were so nicely done. Fresh black mulch seemed to frame the home and plantings everywhere she looked. It was absolutely perfect in her eyes. The girls squealed with delight. They loved it, and a usually disinterested Raheem even seemed a bit excited about what he was seeing.

"Nana, I love it," both Kia and Keema had said. Keisha was somewhere off in Tito's shadow. She had been drifting away from home more and more with each passing day. Mother Porter would not be chasing her. She had seen the same signs twice in her own daughters and chasing only made them run. This time with her granddaughter she would not chase.

When Mother Porter entered the home she moved quickly to the kitchen. She looked over the kitchen as if it were some sort of holy sanctuary. In truth, it was her sanctuary within her home. But before she could take in the details of the kitchen she was flooded with other thoughts. As she pondered the situation she started to wonder whether it really felt right. Was it right for the family to accept such an elaborate gift, solely predicated on the back of her grandson's athletic abilities calculated for the future? Raheem was clearly her favored grandchild, no matter how much she had denied it to all who called her out about the matter in the past. Mother Porter felt worried instead of joy about the recent good fortune. "It's founded on a lie," she thought, and then began to worry even more. "What if her grandson were to begin to get pestered about the family's finances? For Christ's sake, Raheem, although approaching 6'7" and one sandwich away from 240 pounds was still not yet 17 years of age. That is a lot of pressure for a young man." Finally, she made her decision. She would not go further with this charade.

"Raheem," Mother Porter called out to him. She watched as the man-child of a grandson came toward the kitchen. It had been a few days since seeing him with so much business accruing. As Raheem walked into the kitchen it hit her. She became mindful of the fact that her grandson was growing much taller and wider. With that realization, she thought of him living in such a small basement. The basement, wow...it hit her; she began to feel guilt about her giant of a grandson squeezing into such a tight space shared with the washing machine and hot humid dryer. For a moment she fixed her gaze on this young man who had developed the maturity of a man twice his age.

"Nana," she came to.

"Yes Baby."

"Come on, I want to show you Gonzo's area out in the huge back yard."

"We leaving that greedy mutt with the corner boys on 9th Street," Mother Porter playfully said. The two walked outside together and then strolled the perimeters of the acre-and-a-half in the rear of the home as they talked. Grandmother and grandson...it was like a Hallmark Card.

"Raheem, you know your Nana was always worried that you and Kareem would end up working for Tito or someone else on that corner. No matter how well you behaved, I always worried about that."

"Yeah, I know Nana."

"When Kareem got killed last year I kept thinking, what in God's name did I do wrong?"

"You ain't do nothing wrong, Nana."

"Basketball, how could he die doing that?"

"It was a robbery, Nana."

"I know that, but now your Nana's got something else weighing on her heart that I need to share."

"Me and Kareen was really brothers, I always thought that, Nana, it's okay."

"No boy, I don't know about that, I'm talkin bout you."

"Me? What about me, Nana?"

"You, Floyd, all this money business this big house. Now some lady is showing me life insurance policies that Floyd sent for me to sign for you. It's a bit much, Raheem." Mother Porter and Raheem now stopped walking and sat down on a picnic bench which was quite a way back on the property but facing the rear if the house. The grass was freshly cut and gnats were everywhere. Both of them were flailing their arms around their faces in an effort to get rid of the swarms of little pests.

"Gonzo ain't gonna like these bugs, I'll bet that much," Mother Porter said in between the very serious conversation. "You ain't in no pros yet Baby. You ain't got no reason to have all this money, house and I hear you gitten a new big truck or one of the SUVs like Bo." She had a pained look on her face as she struggled to continue. "How in god's name could we possibly explain this stuff to the people if they come?"

Raheem took a few seconds to ingest all of what his wise Grandmother had just laid on him. In all the hype of his street ball games and the murders between the Youngbloods and 9th Street, Joy and Tammy, his SATs, and his driver's license, Raheem had totally forgotten to confer with his only legal guardian about any of this. After all, any benefits or rewards in the future or present were all for her. He simply forgot to ask if she'd even accept them.

"Nana," Raheem said softly, "I just always assumed this was what you wanted. You work seven days a week washing clothes, cooking platters. This is my way of doing my part. I'm not hurting anyone Nana, I'm just playing basketball, that's all."

"I know that Baby, but..."

"Let me finish, Nana," Raheem interrupted. "Me and Kareem dreamed of this. We told you this would happen. You even said that we should keep saying it and it may come true. You taught us that scripture says: 'Life and death was in the power of the tongue.' Well guess what? I believed that stuff you told us as kids, wasn't it true when you said it?"

"Yeah Baby."

"And about them people, what people? We ain't stole nothing, and we ain't sold nothing! If this were five years ago, I would be headed directly to the NBA. Truth is, I act like I don't really understand, but that's all part of the game, Nana. You know me better than that. So let 'them people' come. The most they can discover is we was poor, and now we ain't. Then they take away my scholarship, and that's that. We wait a year or I play in Europe until I'm legally eligible to suit up for an NBA team. Truth be told, I'd rather have it that way. I don't like them college folks. They are more crooked than any drug dealer in the Badlands with twice...no four times the money. So Nana, you keep your house and hang on to the 9th Street house, rent it out if it will make you feel any better, but me and Gonzo livin here!" Raheem grabbed his Grandmom and gave her a big hug and a kiss.

"Oh, I love you sooo much, Raheem. Please, please be careful out there for me," Mother Porter implored as the two walked toward the house. Raheem and his grandmother side-by-side, sun setting in the west as they returned to go back inside.

Chapter 14

It was more noise than Raheem had ever heard before. The high windy pitch of the G4 Lear Jet engines were revving as he and Floyd walked the tarmac. This was all very new territory for Raheem and he was loving every minute. Floyd had immediately sent for the jet once given the green light by the Kozlow couple. With the final championship game still a week away, Floyd decided that he would take his new toy out for a test run. First he would fly to the University of Kansas for an unannounced, unofficial visit. With only a verbal commitment to the school, Floyd didn't want to make too much noise as of yet. He had plans to continue squeezing the slave owners down on Tobacco Row for as much up front bag money as he could possibly get. Simply put, Floyd loved "sticking it to the man!" In some cases, such as Kansas, he got the rare opportunity to stick it to him quite literally. If time permitted while in Kansas for the day, he would jump up and down on Jill Kozlow once more. Floyd smiled at the thought.

In Floyd's mind, this was all perfect pay-back for being looked over when he was a young baller trying like the dickens to make it to a premier University which would have assured him a trip to the NBA. Now, as he sat in the calf skin leather coach seats, in a private jet, preparing to eat freshly caught Live Maine Lobster, and fillet mignon, Blair Silk Floyd had all the financial income as well as the toys to match any current baller in the league. The power to hustle up control over a young baller's future just supported his lifestyle that much more.

The rumbling of the ground as the plane picked up speed gave Floyd comfort. The plane was preparing for take-off. Once in the air, one of the two tall private flight attendants, who looked like she'd been torn out of the pages of a *Victoria's Secret* catalog, began to cater to the only passengers on the plane.

I can't believe we're the only ones on this plane, Floyd," Raheem said as he looked around.

"We have a movie listing too, Mr. Porter," The stewardess said.

"I'm cool, just flip the game on in an hour," Raheem said as he watched the second stewardess roll out the first tray of food.

"We have champagne also, Mr. Floyd, several types."

"I'll have a Rossi with the main course, preferable Moet," Floyd said almost immediately. Floyd was texting several people on two different phones. With each passing day, Floyd's position strengthened. AAU coaches from all over the United States were calling. Coaches were jockeying for favors from Floyd's ranking power. With one phone call, Floyd could now have an unranked high school freshman on the charts within a matter of hours. More than the money that Blair Floyd was raking in, the power was of far more importance. He reeked of power before the major deal with the Kansas businessmen and the Kozlow network. Now with that power nucleus he was firmly cast in this element.

"Listen, Heem, I know what's going on with you and Bo.

"What you mean, Floyd?" Raheem said as he was filling his plate with salad and fruit.

"I know Bo has it in his mind that all of you should continue on at Cincinnati. Well, it ain't gonna happen. If he would have listened, I would have had him at one of the big five. North Carolina, Kansas, Michigan State, Louisville or Kentucky. Then it would have been possible for all of you to play together at the next level. As of now, it looks like it will be you and Malik going to Kansas. If I can somehow get Mill to play a bit bigger in the paint and get his fundamentals together, we can get him a scholarship there also. The assistant coach and I will talk about that at a later date. In the meantime, I need to talk to them both about their SATs. Speaking of which, how are your studies with Joy?" Floyd now preparing to eat his first class fare. Raheem couldn't hide the emotion of lust on his face once Joy's name came up.

"Are you fucking Joy?" Floyd blurted out when he saw Raheem's face.

"Naw, naw, I ain't fucking her Floyd."

"Yeah, well you two are doing something because she gave me the same dumb ass look when I questioned her about your progress. The good thing is that you are really book smart already. At least that is what Joy said. It's just the School District in Philly is running late concerning the curriculum versus the national testing system for college entry. So, in your case, it's not that you're a challenged learner, it's that the system never gave you the advanced courses that would help you ace the test. And that's Joy's job."

"I know Floyd, we've been on it hard. I'm doing good."

"I'm doing well," Floyd shot back. "Um, I'm doing well...that's the proper way to respond."

"Yeah, well I'm doing well," Raheem said.

"Where's my melted butter? Did she put butter on your entrée?" Floyd was looking over the several trays of food for his butter.

"Nope, I don't see it," Raheem said as he smothered his huge steak in sauce.

"How do you feel about Tammy?" Raheem asked.

"What do you mean? Do I like her? I don't fuck my employees, especially the young girls, too much trouble."

"No, is she alright, I mean." Raheem asked,

"Alright in what respect." Floyd was trying to get his young protégé to engage in some intellectual dialogue.

"I mean...is she a smart girl or a good girl or a under-cover...you know?"

"Well, let me give it to you this way. She is my paid intern, I pay all my interns. I won't tell you what school she attends or her major, that's your job to find out. She has never tried to flirt with the boss or worn overly sexy clothes to work like most vying for my attention. She is always on time and is very serious about her work. Finally, she mostly works in my real estate department, but of late, she is learning the business of consulting. She is a very focused young lady with success written all over her personality." At that moment, the attendant brought him a bowl of melted butter and Floyd paused to say, "Thank you."

Raheem was eating his third lobster tail by the end of Floyd's lecture.

"How much do you weigh," Floyd asked as he watched the young eating machine devour piles of food in what seemed like just a few minutes.

"Two-forty-two," Raheem responded.

"I'd like to see you at 250, but not over that. You're what, 6'7" now?"

"Yeah, at my last doctor's appointment."

"Okay, you will probably end up at a three, but if you get too big, pros will expect you to play at the four-position. With your speed and leaping ability I'd like for you to stay at the three. That's why you're going to prep school this year."

"I like Edison, Floyd," Raheem protested.

"Of course you do, with all them pretty Rican girls all over you. That ain't nothing, you'll have those same girls after you no matter where you are. However if you stay in that system this year, your college prep courses are in jeopardy as well as your fundamentals. The coach there will have you playing center," Floyd said with disgust.

"Mill is playing center," Raheem continued his weak rebuttal.

"You're going prep, Raheem, and that's it. Now if both Malik and Mill act right, I'll transfer them also. I could room all three of you together in a townhouse out in West Chester in Chester County."

"Why so far?" Raheem asked.

"That's where the school is. And, it won't be far from your new house with your Grandmom."

"Will we play Chester High?"

"No, they're in Delaware County and fuck Chester High. They're high-school kids. Prep schools are made up teams of the very best in the country. Your schedule will consist of nationally ranked school only."

"Chester's always ranked," Raheem said.

"Yeah, well they had better get a bigger road schedule if they want a piece of the national spotlight," Floyd stated as if it was a simple matter of fact.

Chapter 15

Bo's Revenge

Back in Philadelphia Bo was setting his plans up to conquer the basketball world. He had made his position perfectly clear. He didn't trust Blair Floyd, he didn't like Blair Floyd and now he was out to expose Blair Floyd. It wasn't enough that he had stolen his best friend and ruined plans for the two to play ball at the same university. He was now planning on stealing both Mill and Malik. Before the summer had hit, Bo was very carefully working out his strategy for ensuring that his entire crew would attend Cincy. Alone, each player was probably an above average Division IA college player, save Bo and Raheem. However, as a team the five they were a clear favorite to win a national DI title. Not since the 1984-85 Dobbins Tech team with Hank "the Bank" Gathers and Bo Kimble had high school ballers been this celebrated. Simply put, Bo needed his younger counterparts to fulfill his vision in the coming years. He had envisioned a team not unlike the great Georgetown teams of the 1980s or a Fab Five of Michigan in the 1990s; only better. Not just one, but two or maybe three titles. All five would eventually head off into the sunset of the N.B.A. First round. The entire starting five, for the first time in history. One through five, right down the line. Off course, Bo would be picked #1. Sure Raheem was a human highlight film and everyone loved him, but with time, pro teams would come to see that it was Bohemian Johnson who made everyone play at the higher level.

Bo had his fantasy. Without him, most players were simply good, but with him at the point guard position and steering at the helm, other players played magnificently. That's how he saw it. But for right now, he had to somehow stop Floyd and his evil plan. Bo had taken money and gifts. He was given a new SUV through a family member and his mother was also moved out of the Badlands area into a new development bordering on the Schuylkill River in South Philadelphia. Bo understood all of this to be in the clear violation of his NCAA rules. That didn't matter at all to him. He would find a way to burn Floyd, and if Raheem didn't play fair, he would burn him too. This was war and in war no man is safe!

"Bo, Bo, Bo," she cried out to him but Bo was both angry and in deep concentration. He could neither hear nor feel the young Keema's pain. He had taken the entire Viagra and now he could not bust his nut. He had the young Keema's face smashed down in a pillow with a tight grip on the back of her neck. With her young perky ass hiked up in the air, Bo pounded her very wet pussy.

"This is my pussy, you hear me! This is mine! You better not ever give this pussy away," Bo verbally scolded the young Keema.

"Bo, you hurtin me," Keema cried in vain. This wasn't about sexual satisfaction, it wasn't even about Keem's fine teenaged ass. It was about power, validation and total disrespect. The young Keema made Bo feel dominant and in his constant narcissistic state, he needed validation all the time. And, because Raheem had now sided with Floyd, fucking his young sister and cousin was the ultimate means of disrespect.

"I'm gone fuck you all day long," Bo pounded the young Keema until he was totally exhausted. An hour later he had finally come. The bed in his air conditioned room was totally drenched in both sweat and blood. Keema lay on her stomach crying uncontrollably. Bo finally got to his feet. He looked at the violated Keema, then walked out of the bedroom without a word. He returned a few minutes later.

"Get in the shower and then put one of these on," throwing a box of Kotex in her direction. Keema got up and reached out to Bo.

"What, you want a hug?" Bo said in disgust. Then he barked at Keema again, "I gotta wash the Got Damn sheets before my mom get home. Get in the shower!"

Keema had always liked Bo and thought that he liked her too. "One day Bo is gonna ask me to be his girl, you wait and see," Keema had boasted to Kia on several occasions while the two lay in bed at night.

"Bo don't like you girl, he likes grown women in they 20s."

"Yeah well, that ain't what his eyes say. I always catch him lookin when I walk by in the living room. And once I saw him whispering to Malik and smile after I went up the steps."

"You got a fat butt dummie, all boys gonna look and wish. Like Nana said, just cause a man want some, don't mean that he want you!"

Those words of wisdom couldn't have rung louder at that moment. Keema realized that Bo didn't want her. He moved her all about the bedroom like old furniture then tossed her aside like trash. The condom Keema handed Bo was tossed to the side of the bed after faking like he had put it on. When Keema realized that he was raw, she tried to protest.

Bo simply over-powered her and threw her young legs behind her head. "Shut up and take this dick!"

Now sore and broken, Keema wished that she had taken the advice of her sister.

Chapter 16

Fanfare

The school visit may have been unofficial and Floyd and Raheem had three more schools to fly out to see on their route. Even with most of the students away on summer break the fanfare was as if the President was making a visit to the beautifully manicured expansive campus.

"I thought no one knew we were coming," a smiling Raheem said as the two were greeted by a beautiful blond-haired tall female student. There were no staff in sight.

"Hi, I'm Amy and this is Kat," pointing to the shorter of the two blonds.

"I'm Raheem Porter," Raheem said in awe of the welcome from all of the student's that surrounded him.

"We know, silly," Amy said and Kat echoed the same. The cheerleaders behind them were all jockeying for position to meet the nationally famous high school phenom. Raheem very patiently shook the hands of each and every student. Floyd quietly snuck off leaving the young baller to his own devices.

"Come on, Raheem, you belong to me and Kat for the day. You are our guest." Raheem listened and broke out in a broad smile as he followed the two young college co-eds. They very easily and happily walked about the entire campus picking up a few female friends along the way. Once they entered the huge sports arena Raheem was off into space.

"This is Jayhawk country. The history was evident. The banners were lined high in the rafters. Conference Championships and National titles. Kansas had deep history concerning basketball.

"Raheem, did you know Wilt Chamberlain attended our University," Kat happily said. "And, he too was a Philadelphian," Amy interjected with her bubbly personality shining through.

"Yes, I'm very familiar with our connection," Raheem said as he looked about the sacred ground of Danny Manning and the Great Wilt the Stilt. "Where the basketballs?" Raheem asked as he looked around towards the corners of the arena floor. With that, the very meticulous Amy turned to give a young freshman a non-verbal order. He ran off to retrieve a ball without being told.

As Raheem walked around the wooden floor which shined like glass, Amy and Kat continued their memorized spiel. Raheem was stomping and sliding his size 14½ sneakers across the floor in what appeared to be a test of the footing.

"Here's the ball Raheem," the smiling freshman said as he returned to the arena floor, now totally out of breath. He threw the ball to the living teenaged legend and, on one bounce, Raheem dunked it without effort for the small college crowd. They all clapped and cheered. Amy and Kat stayed close by Raheem, almost as if they were his body-guards. Amy was chatting on and on about the school programs and the deep history of the University. The focal point at the moment was civil rights. Amy was explaining how the University was one of the first to welcome African-American students on campus during the Jim Crow South era. Raheem had long since drifted off into his own world. He was in the arena with his father figure.

"You are prime for a place like this. This building has a lot of history son. It has graced the presence of all the great college ball players of the past."

"Yeah, I know, Dad," Raheem softly said while he dribbled the ball between his legs and took a jump shot. *Swish* was the only sound heard at the end of the ball's arc toward the basket. "But Dad, shouldn't I at least consider some of the other great schools?"

"Sure, why not visit them, check their arenas out, see what the campuses feel like to you, but I think this place is a safe haven for you. It's far away from the daily drama of the inner city."

Raheem took another shot. *Swish.* "Thanks Dad, I love you."

"You do? I love you too," Amy said holding her mouth and jumping up and down with Kat. "Don't you love me too, Raheem?" Kat asked with hopeful eyes staring directly at him.

"Sure I do," Raheem said as he gave the pint sized blonde a hug. Raheem had made the two students glow with his small simple gesture of a man twice his age. Raheem was not only maturing as a man in size with each passing day, his mind was growing in wisdom.

***

Floyd and Raheem were back on the plane and now headed to North Carolina. Floyd was a bit reluctant to make such a trip after giving the verbal commitment to Kansas University. He was well aware of just how beautiful North Carolina was as a state and how pretty the campus was too. The air in North Carolina is even better than in the North. The beautiful trees, lawns and historical buildings all act as bait to capture high school super stars. Duke, North Carolina, NC State and Wake Forest. They all lined up on Tobacco Row. Remnants of a time long ago. The slave owners of the South. Floyd couldn't have cared less when he was in high school. Once he was stepped over in his senior year, all that changed. From now on he would do business with all big business moguls as if he were a ghost from slavery's past. "Fuck that! I'm no house nigger nor field nigger; I'm the New Nigger. I'm here on behalf of all my ancestors to collect reparations," Floyd thought to himself and smiled at his own wit...

Chapter 17

"I don't like it Bo," Moop said to his life-long friend after hearing the beginning of his plans to destroy Floyd, sabotage Raheem's college career and maybe totally ruin it for good. "It just don't seem right, Bo." Moop almost begging Bo to reconsider his plans.

"And, I'm fuckin his sister, next I'm a fuck his cousin," Bo said with distain showing on his face and his mouth twisted up on one side of his face.

"You what? Are you crazy, Bo?"

"And that tight young girl pussy is good! I bet Kia's is even better."

"Man, I'm not having this conversation with you. You done lost it Bo. That's Raheems' people we talkin bout." Moop now had tears in his eyes after hearing about the blatant disrespect and disregard for their friend.

"What you with them, fat boy?" The two were in the hot and humid gym on 4th and Fairmount Avenue. Moop had a basketball under his huge arm. They were there to simply practice but it had now turned deathly ugly. "Damn man, that's how we talk to each other now?" Moop spoke with some fire in his voice but he was visibly hurt.

"What? You are fat! And you are always out of shape. You two steps late on most plays. You gas out by the third quarter and your fat ass ain't smart enough to play a zone defense. The only reason I wanted you at Cincy with me was to keep that bitch ass Raheem happy"

Bo had never hurled insults at Moop, never. Moop dropped the ball and walked out of the gym.

Later in the evening a young Kia was making the short walk from June's hospital room at Temple University Hospital to 9th and Indiana. The house was a ghost of its usual self because of the move to Kennett Square in the burbs. Kia had plans for Keisha to pick her up later in the evening and to drive her home after she sold all of Mother Porter's pies.

As Kia began to walk down Germantown Avenue she was spotted by Bo. "Kia, Kia," followed by a beeping horn. But Kia was deep in a lovers stupor from the visit with June. The two had finally confessed their emotional bond and their physical attraction. June had even made a proclamation–albeit a weak-sounding one–about his exit from selling drugs and returning to high school. Kia reveled in the idea of this change. She would tutor him herself, she had boldly stated. And after high school, they would attend college together and with their skills as a cook and June's business sense, the two would start a restaurant. Kia left out the part about marriage. She wanted June to come up with that idea on his own.

"Kia, Kia!"

"Oh, hi, Bo," Kia finally gave him recognition and walked toward his SUV.

"Where you going cutie," Bo shouted out.

"I'm headed to the house to sell the pies, then I'm going home with Keisha."

"Yeah, I heard about the new house in Chester County; I hear it's really nice," Bo sounded genuinely happy for Kia's family.

"I absolutely love it," Kia said as the two pulled up in front of the door.

"I see the cops left but that the big mobile station is still here."

"Yeah I guess the station is supposed to have some sort of deterrent. It's had very little effect as you can see." Kia said just as two dope fiends walk past, one with his "works" in his hand heading toward the graveyard.

"Who's in the house?" Bo asked

"Nobody, or there shouldn't be anyone. Nanna is at work I got a check on the pies and platters."

"Y'all still doing that shit, with all the money you *got* now," Bo said as Kia opened the gated screen doors and unlocked the second door.

"What money? Shit these pies is our money; Nana is always doing extra work. She washes in the summer because it pays more. This cooking pays all kinds of bills. Nana says we ain't never given this up. It sustained us all these years so why stop cooking now? She gets $15 a pie in the new neighborhood we live in going door-to-door."

"What? Y'all niggers done took this ghetto shit out to Chester County? Them white folks gone vote y'all black asses the fuck out of they county you watch."

Kia's young eyes opened wide at those words. "They could do that?"

"Hell yeah, white people is some shit like that. They put that shit on the ballot and vote your black asses right out of the county and back to the Badlands. They did that shit down south somewhere, I saw it on Oprah." Bo sounded very convincing.

"No they can't. I'm gonna ask my Nanna." Kia began to set the pies on the table in the front room and started to re-heat the food platters. Bo watched her every move like a hawk. He watched her cute ripe body as she glided about the kitchen like a professional.

"Where's your brother?" Bo clearly knew where Raheem was but decided to ask anyway.

"He's either in Kansas or North Carolina. Him and Floyd few out yesterday early in the morning. They will be back tomorrow night. Y'all got the championship game on 16th Street?

"Yeah, that would bring the two high rollers back home," Bo said. Kia could sense a bit of discontent in his voice.

"Why you say it like that?"

"Naw, I'm just saying. They flying high, that's all." Kia excused herself to use the bathroom. Once she ran up the steps, Bo immediately locked the front door. After locking the door he began to climb the stairs to the small row house. The hallway bathroom door was slightly ajar. Bo watched through the mirror as the young Kia prepared to wipe herself after peeing. Bo was now fully aroused. Before she could pull her pants and panties up, Bo swung open the door.

Kia jerked her head up quickly; "Bo, what you doin, get out of here," she yelled. She could see that Bo had fire in his eyes as he grabbed Kia roughly by her arm. She hopped a bit because her pants were still down around her ankles. She placed one hand on the wall to stop the pulling from Bo. When he realized this counter-move, he scooped the petite Kia up over his shoulders, holding her legs with one arm and bracing her bare backside with the other. Bo carried Kia into the bare bedroom that was furnished with, of all things, a mattress. Bo body-slammed the small Kia down on the bed once he realized that she was unwilling to comply. The slam, even on a mattress, had knocked the wind out of Kia. She moaned in pain. Bo could see that his prey was wounded so he quickly undressed then pulled Kia's pants completely off.

He was having trouble with her white cotton panties so he just ripped them off with one hard pull and then another.

"Why you doin this, Bo?" Kia was crying.

"Shut up and open your legs or I'm gonna get rough." Kia reluctantly complied.

"Bo, I'm a virgin," Kia whimpered when it appeared that Bo was having a very difficult time entering her tight vagina. At that, Bo became even more determined, grunting in Kia's ear at the mere word "virgin." His large penis had finally released enough pre-cum to lubricate its way in.

"Ahh," Bo sighed in Kia's ear from primal pleasure while Kia simultaneously screamed in pain—more psychological than physical—with the clear notion that her prize possession, the only thing that she truly had savored for her one true love, was now gone. Gone to a boy that she had looked up to as a big brother. And as Bo humped and humped on top of her, grunting and mumbling incoherently, Kia thought about June. June would have been gentle with her.

"Turn over," Bo growled while physically moving the young Kia himself. Kia was not there, she was reading a book to her real love. Back at Temple Hospital. "Damn, this pussy is good," Bo stated as he pulled on Kia's hair from behind, bringing her out of her dream. Now, feeling the pain, Kia began to cry.

"Yeah, I know, I know I'm almost finished though. Bo kissed Kia's cheek as if to give a show of affection. A few more minutes passed and Bo finally came. "Huh, huh," two last hard releasing strokes as he transferred his life into her. The final indignity. Bo stumbled to his feet. "Got damn, y'all bleed in this family. You bleed more than Keema," as he looked at the bed. Kia was wondering whether to believe her ears: Keema? Did Bo rape her also? Kia got up to go into the bathroom. Bo was standing tall and proud of himself as he peed into the toilet.

"Damn Kia, you got some good pussy, girl. Kia turned on the water for the tub and stepped in. Bo was talking to her as if everything was fine. Kia began to wash herself. Bo, still naked, looked at her from behind, got excited and picked Kia up an half-dragged her back to the bedroom once more. Bo raped Kia for the rest of the afternoon...

Chapter 18

"Oh yeah, I see. How are you making out? I'd like to keep this away from Raheem as long as possible if we can. I know Moop, I realize you're only looking out for your brothers and teammates. Just keep this to yourself until things can get worked out. I will talk to you tomorrow I got good news for you, okay? Alright, peace," and with those words Floyd clicked his phone and took a long sip of the white sparkling wine. "Give me something stronger, please," Floyd said to the waitress in almost a whisper just a Raheem returned to the table from using the restroom.

The two, mentor and student, had endured a very long few days. They were thoroughly entertained by the Tar Heels finest and several other schools in the region were waiting and hoping that, for some reason, the basketball gods would smile on them and Raheem Porter would, at the very least, pay their school a short visit.

NC State and Wake Forrest were both on the agenda and Floyd was finally convinced to stop by when two local boosters showed up at his and Raheem's hotel with blank checks as well as cash. Of course Floyd insisted that there simply wasn't enough time to visit and he hoped he could find time in the future. At the moment of separation, somehow $25,000 per visit was agreed upon. There was also an understanding of $250,000 if the young player would commit. The conversation was basically repeated with the other booster/local businessman. Schools such as Davidson and East Carolina simply didn't stand a change.

"Wake Forrest is nice, don't you think Floyd?"

"Yeah, it's alright."

"Plus I hear that point guard, um what's his name, is headed there," a very jubilant Raheem stated. "I really wanted to visit Duke though Floyd."

"Yeah I know, but their coach teaches and coaches a college-only style--team game. With your body and athletic play, you would never fit into his system."

"Yeah? Why not Floyd?"

"Well some kids are just given talent that can't be explained. At a school like Duke nobody's bigger than the system and, trust me Raheem, you would have problems in that system. Kinda like wearing a pair of pants that are way too small."

"The part that Floyd refused to say was the fact that no one had stepped up to the plate for Duke; nobody was willing to pay. "Blue Devils huh, more like Blue Angels," Floyd quietly thought.

"What's next Floyd," an excited Raheem said as he looked over the menu."

"I was thinking maybe we should head back to Philly tonight. This way we are well rested for tomorrow night's game," Floyd spoke calmly but he sounded somewhat distant.

Carlito Ewell

"Sure Floyd, I'm good with that, plus I need to get some running in. I feel heavy from these last few days," Raheem said as he searched Floyd's face for whatever emotion he might be feeling.

The two ate and headed to the private executive airport in Durham, North Carolina. Floyd was serious and focused. Raheem, on the other hand, was very talkative and bright-eyed about the amazing trip. "Yeah Floyd, I think you were right about Kansas. It's a safe environment for me. Plus it is basketball country year round, that's for sure. Them big white boys can play out there. How you think they learned the game like that, Floyd"

"What do you mean?" Floyd said almost robotically, with thought clearly elsewhere.

"I mean, we come up in the hood. Basketball is our life. It's always fast, hard and rough. Guys get killed over a bad foul. Out in the country they ain't killing each other over no bad fouls.," Raheem stated.

"Well, how would you know that?" Floyd asked.

"Because I ain't never heard of it, they live soft out there. It's all safe," Raheem said.

"Yeah well, you remember this, we don't really know what goes on in another man's back yard. You might think he grew up soft, but I know from experience that there ain't no place safe. So always mind your manners in another man's back yard, Raheem. Conduct yourself with respect, firm yeah, but respectful at all times Raheem."

"Yeah, I know Floyd, I know."

Floyd had the stewardess pour him a glass of scotch. Raheem watched the tape of Georgetown versus Villanova while Floyd leaned back in his

116

seat and collected his thoughts. He wanted to be certain that he didn't make any missteps while on his next move dealing with the problem that had just been presented to him over the phone. He most certainly didn't want Raheem emotionally involved or invested in the future problem...

Chapter 19

Tito picked up the phone on the second ring. He listened to the hysterical voice on the other end. He was his usual calm self. "Just be cool, just be cool. Are you sure that's how it went down? Alright then, we'll deal with it." Tito clicked off his cell phone and resumed eating the plate of food in front of him.

"Who was that, Pop?" Keisha asked as she refilled Tito's tall glass with palcha.

"Don't worry about it," Tito quietly said as he picked up his glass with his left hand and grabbed Keisha around her waist with his right arm.

"Alright, I'll act like that when I get a call," Keisha said.

"You stay in your place," Tito said now sounding a bit more serious.

***

Kia sat beside June's bed in Temple University Hospital. Neither said a word. The air in the room was filled with silence. June was staring at the ceiling with murder in his eyes. His skin looked red hot but it was anger and not a high temperature that was causing his blood to boil. Kia was quietly crying. Just 24 hours earlier she had finally admitted her secret feelings and she had also–in the midst of a heavy and deep discourse–given clues concerning her chastity. June didn't need clues or to be told. He had lived on 9th Street his entire young life. He was well aware of who the whores were and who the good girls were. Kia was by far the latter. There was none more pure on the entire block. On many occasions June checked with his shift workers concerning her. Everyone knew that Kia was June's wife, even if the two had not yet formally committed to each other.

Today was a very sad day for them both. "Did you tell your Grandmom?"

"No," Kia said.

"Did you tell Raheem?"

"Hell no, it would break his heart. He may even kill him if he found out. Then what would my family do?" Kia voice quivered with both her anger and her frustration.

"Yeah well, I get out of here tomorrow."

"Please June, I don't want nothing bad to happen to you. Why you always gotta be out front. If you end up in prison, I would die inside," Kia pleaded.

"Cool out, cool out," June said. "Come here, girl." June pulled on Kia's arm gently. He very gingerly scooted over in the hospital bed and guided Kia to lay beside him. The two young lovers very quietly held each other until June's visiting hours were over.

Chapter 20

Championship Night

The night was alive with energy that was electric. It was the final night of summer basketball for 16th Street. Tomorrow would be the start of the AAU season for teenagers. As usual, the summer league was a clear success for the City of Philadelphia. It had brought common folk and celebrities alike to watch Philly's street ballers do their thing. The very popular show *"And 1"* had even shown a great deal of interest in the league. The final night had all of the defeated teams return for a proper awards ceremony. The awards were handed out by the Mayor himself.

Sad Eyes had received the "Legends Award" for his years as a top-level street baller. Woody Wood from 21st and Norris received the "Sixth Man of the Year." The All Stars were as follows: At point guard the one position went to Bad Foot Wood from North Philly. At the two the "shooting guard" went to Bo. The three position, small forward, went to none other than Sad Eyes. The crowd all stood and gave the legend his props once more. At the four position, the power forward, Willie Mack from Northern Liberties took his bow and center, the five, went to Marques Taylor from South Philly.

Raheem was a bit puzzled that he had not won any position. However, he had played the one through four positions the entire tournament so one might surmise that he hadn't established himself enough at any one spot to be awarded. Just when Raheem and his team prepared to take the floor for their championship run, the Mayor spoke: "Now hold on everyone, you don't think we forgot our young superstar. How could we ever do that?" The Mayor was grinning broadly as he made the announcement and the crowd rose to their feet and began to chant, "Ra-Heem, Ra-Heem, Ra-Heem," as if he were a prize fighter preparing to do battle. The embarrassed Raheem was totally stunned. He looked over his shoulder at Floyd who gave his young protégé the nod of approval.

"This is your time man, get used to it. It's just the beginning...Ra-Heem; the outstanding player and most valuable player of the year, Raheem Porter," the Mayor yelled into the mic and the crowd went wild as the young baller bounced to his feet to run over and shake the Mayor's outstretched hand. It took a full 15 minutes for the crowd to settle down and the DJ to stop playing hard bass-pounding music of *Young Money Hit Makers* before the tip-off. Then the Lakers from the Badlands and Sad Eyes part II commenced.

Bo was in very good spirits although once more his younger friend had outshined him. At least he was the best at his position. Bo was a bit pissed that he hadn't won at the point guard position, but the way he saw it he was the best guard no matter what. One or two.

All parties realized that this game would be much more difficult than the last. Sad Eyes had made a coaching change. He got rid of his long-time coach and hired on an old head named Bub from Norris Street. Bub had more championships in the Pennsylvania Prison System than the next five closest coaches combined. He had just made parole after 25 years and the way Sad Eyes saw it, "If he could coach killers to championships, he could damn sure coach us." And he was correct.

Bub was old school, he liked man-on-man defense. "If you can't stick your man then you don't belong in the game. Yeah, I heard about this boy Raheem. Let's make him beat us. Stop the other four players at all costs. And if Raheem drives, foul his young ass extremely hard. Let's win this thing."

On the other end, the stoic Floyd was very cool and collected when he presented his game strategy. "On defense, let's stay with the two three. We're much bigger in the paint as well as up top. Therefore we make them put it to us if they want to score. On offense, Bo, you play the point, Heem, you play the two-three. Move without the ball. If you feel something sweet, then bang out down low. Moop you're at the power; Malik and Mill can both rotate in and out as big men down low. Let's run them off the court. Badlands on three: One-two-three, BADLANDS!"

The tip-off went to Mill and he immediately passed it to Bo on the run. Raheem was out just like old times. Bo faked the pass to Malik on the left and no-look lobbed it to Raheem for the stretched out, one-handed right-hand dunk. The crowd was once again at its feet. The college kids from Temple as well as their team were all on hand even though it was their summer break. This was why they all came. Raheem was now a national phenom. Two weeks away from his 17th birthday and he was playing as if he were a seasoned pro for the NBA.

"That's okay, he has to do that all night to us in order for them to win," Bub yelled from his sideline. Sad Eyes swished the easy two from the top of the left hash mark. "That's your pick-up Bo," Floyd said as the team headed the other way in transition. Raheem was like a rabbit. His lightening quick movement without the ball was a thing of amazement.

Sure there had been many before him that made a career of doing just that. Reggie Miller, Allen Iverson, Ray Allen, just to name a few. That being said, none of them weighed 240 pounds. He was a Mack truck with Maserati speed. "Swish" Raheem answered from the far baseline on the three point line.

"Make sure you put a hand up. Don't just let him pop shots like ducks in a barrel," Bub was a bit more concerned with the easy shot given to Raheem. Although he had planned on making Raheem beat them by buckling down on the other four players, that didn't mean that they should let Raheem simply shoot at will. Even with Bub's experience and his plan of action, he had yet to see a player of Raheem's sheer power and raw athleticism. Before this night would end, he too would believe.

The game was very competitive but somewhat basically fundamental. The score was tied at 28. Then as if a switch had turned on, Raheem picked Sad Eyes and took flight toward his basket. Instead of taking a straight path, Raheem took the right side and launched toward the rim with a one-handed tuck rock the cradled dunk–vintage Jordan 1987. The look on Raheem's face was of a man on a mission now. For the next five possessions he refused to pass the ball. He placed his team on his back and gave a show to the Philadelphia crowd of epic proportion. Three-pointers back-to-back. He waited for the double team, followed with a give and go for the tomahawk dunk.

What began as a very competitive display of round ball, ended in an utter and complete blowout! The Championship was taken by the Badland Lakers. There were congratulations all around. The music blared through the huge flat-black speakers supplied by Power 99. College recruits, pro scouts, go-go girls and grandmothers, were all on hand. They all understood that they had witnessed something very special, something that they'd be talking about for years to come. The party seemed to be headed to an all-nighter.

"Listen, get your stuff, we gonna blow," Floyd instructed.

"Where is Bo," Raheem asked.

"Yeah, well, we need to have a talk about him tomorrow. He's been up to no good. I didn't want to tell you before the game."

"Like what?" Raheem questioned as he grabbed his bag and began to follow Floyd to the waiting vehicle being driven by one of Floyd's office assistants.

"Ah shit, you don't need this. Let me deal with him and we'll talk about it." The two jumped into the SUV and headed out. Meanwhile, Bo was in his SUV with Prince and Willie Mack.

"What yall gone do," Bo asked.

"I'm gone take a shower and head to the Ben Franklin Plaza. They having the after-party there," Will said.

Prince spoke up, "I might ride with you, Will."

"Yeah, well, I'll meet yall there later. I'm gone hit this young girl first, then I'll head out. I leave for Cincy in two more days," Bo said with excitement in his voice. After dropping off the two team mates at the corner of 6th and Parrish Streets, he hung a right on Fairmount Avenue and headed toward Broad. Once he got to Broad Street, instead of making a left and going to I-76 and then towards home, he made the fatal mistake of going right to stop at McDonalds on Girard Avenue.

Bo made the right turn off of Broad Street into McDonald's parking lot and then decided to use the drive-thru. Before he could pull up, a low riding Chevy truck cut him off to go before him. "What the fuck? Stupid Ricans." Bo pulled in and ordered at the mic. He then turned up Tupac's Machiavelli's "Hail Mary" and sang along. A truck pulled in behind him and flashed his high-beams. The bright lights made him turn around and look over his shoulder. "What the fuck is going on tonight," Bo said to himself. Then as he turned back around he sensed a figure beside his car but it all happened so fast, his brain didn't have time to interpret what he was sensing.

"Eat that nigga." Blaaaw, a shot rang out and Bo fell sideways out of his driver's-sidedoor. The killer shot once more to the back of his head. The truck behind Bo pushed his SUV out of the way, making Bo's lifeless body fall out into its path. The driver of the ensuing truck drove right over the lifeless body of Bohemian Johnson. The weight of the truck and the huge wheels spinning separated his torso from the lower half of his body. The back wheels then crushed what was left of his skull. His final indignity.

When the homicide unit showed up with the meat wagon, they had pictures taken. Bo's body was so torn into pieces that the scene looked fake, almost as if a movie director had a poor special effects team. It took until late in the afternoon of the following day to find the lower half of Bo's jaw. The jaw had been stuck in the rubber tread of one of the tires of the big truck. A witness said that the driver very calmly got out of the truck and kicked something. That something was the lower half of Bo's jaw...

Chapter 21

Floyd was showered and now listening to the smooth sounds of Chuck Mangione's alto saxophone. He had received the call before he parked his car and took the elevator to his condo. One of his maids had his steam 12-head shower prepped to exactly 101 degrees Fahrenheit. Floyd undressed in his fully Italian marbled bath and shower room. His coffee-toned maid picked up each item as it hit the floor. Floyd turned to step into the large shower as the steam rushed out into the cool bathroom.

"Ahhh," Floyd exhaled as he dropped his head back allowing the hot water direct contact with his face from above. He turned his head from side-to-side and then slowly bent over with his head down and rested both hands on his knees as he allowed the hot water time to work on his tired back. Floyd very flexibly stretched his hands to his feet and then placed both palms flat on the shower floor. As he slowly began to rise up his beautiful maid opened the shower door and stepped in with her long dark silky hair and her very ample lower half. No words were spoken; she simply began lathering Floyd's back and legs as he continued to slowly stretch.

After shower, the maid had Floyd's snifter ready with his aged cognac. Floyd placed the huge Championship Trophy in front of the fireplace. He stared at it as his maid massaged his legs and feet. Floyd slowly stroked the long silky hair of his servant. He was safe. In his business account safely tucked away was seven million dollars. In his office safe rested $500,000 in cash from the Kozlows and in his bedroom safe another million that he had earned from his trip down south. Sure three different boosters from three different schools would be upset with Floyd for a while, but he had a stable of good ball players now and many more were calling. Fathers lobbying for their sons, especially once word got out that his team had won the Philly Street Ball Classic. Raheem Porter was a special case, but Floyd now had his eyes set on an eighth-grader named James Parker out of Chi-town. With the AAU coming up, he would put Raheem on a big city restriction. No Philly, period. It's just too dangerous. People are just way too jealous. Get Raheem through his final year of school and off to Kansas. Maybe by then, Tammy would be prepared to make a step up to manager. "That would be perfect. Have Tammy manage Raheem with me controlling everything behind closed doors." Floyd smiled at the thought. Thirteen percent of 100 million. Real simple math, 13 million. "Shit, at least 100 million of endorsements for Raheem," Floyd thought to himself a grinned once more.

"Te gusta."

"Si."

"To mar me."

"Ahora Mismo?" Floyd asked.

"Si, Popi, Si." And with that, Floyd followed his beautiful dark-skinned voluptuous lover to this bedroom...

***

"Nooo, nooo,' Raheem yelled from his bedroom the following morning. Mother Porter was cooking breakfast in her huge new kitchen when she heard Raheem cry out. The yelling woke up Keema and she ran toward Raheem's room. Kia lay awake in her bed; she very quietly began to sob. No one needed to tell her what the trouble was. She immediately picked up her cell phone and called June.

Back in Raheem's bedroom, Mother Porter tried in vain to find out why Raheem was crying. She picked up his phone; it was Moop on the other end. "Mother?"

"What happen Baby," she gently asked with Raheem sobbing face down in his pillow.

"They killed Bo last night after the game. They killed him at McDonald's at Broad and Girard.

"That was him? I saw that on the news last night, good God almighty. Let me tend to my grandson."

"Okay Mother, I'll call later."

Mother Porter hugged her huge grandson around his head as he sobbed like a baby. Keema held her grandmother around her waist as she sobbed. Kia was in her bedroom.

"June?"

"Yeah."

"You Okay?" Kia sounded concerned.

"Yeah, I'm good, how bout you," June said in an even tone.

"I mean, are you okay," Kia asked once more.

"Yeah, I get out of here today," June said with a tone of agitation.

"You been there at the hospital all night?"

"Kia, I just told you I'm outta here today, are you coming?"

"Yes, yes I'm coming, June. I love you, I love you," Kia cried over the phone uncontrollably.

"Yo, are you cool, Ma? I told you I am gonna take care of you, you'll be alright, just calm down," June said.

'Okay as soon as Keisha get here I'll be there," Kia said. "And first I'm gonna teach you how to drive," Kia tried to laugh over her sobs. Once she hung up she slowly waked into her brother's room. She silently stood at the door and watched her family. She thought to herself of all the pain that Bo had caused. She was sure that he was dead. No one had told her yet, but she somehow instinctively knew it. She saw her cousin crying and could see Bo, tall and strong, ripping at her clothes, entering her with that look on his face. Grunting in her ear as she begged for him to stop. Then if that weren't enough, he'd walk around the house naked after using the toilet and freely getting a cold drink out from the fridge, standing there naked, flashing his penis around the house like feathers on a peacock. The audacity of him to talk to her so crudely about her vagina. And after he had enough he acted as if he had done her some favor. Well fuck him! I hope he is burning in hell right now with a hot rod up in his rectum. I'm not gonna cry for him. Kia wiped her face, turned and left the room...

Chapter 22

Tito picked up his phone and simply listened. When the caller was finished he clicked off without uttering one word. He then followed the 10 or so others along with Kia and Keisha as they walked June into the house. The place looked like a party store with red and silver mylar balloons floating in front of the house, leading into the front door and bouncing off of the living room ceiling. Everywhere you looked, balloons, which although a bit tacky, did seem to help create a joyful and festive mood. Everyone including Tito was very happy that June had come through this ordeal unscathed. The house was crowded with visitors coming and going all day. The mobile police station had left several days earlier so the corner was popping once more.

One of June's workers gave him a large brown paper bag. "What's this," June asked.

"It's your shift money from the last two-and-a-half weeks, Pop."

"Good lookin Yo," June said without looking into the bag. Not long after this exchange, two men came into the house. They were fairly stocky black men but Kia could tell by their clothing and their mannerisms that they were *hibaros,* Spanish for hick or hillbilly. They spoke first with Tito, whispering in his ear on either side. Then they paid their respects to June, shaking his hand one at a time. Then they each whispered something into June's ear. June responded with something in a Spanish dialect that was unfamiliar to Kia. A mountain term, unique only to his family's home town back on the island. The two men then turned to June's mother and said, "Bendicion," one after the other. She blessed them both and they quietly left...

The homicide detectives were sitting in Floyd's office when he finally strolled into work. As usual he had both cell phones going at once. Both were pressed to opposite sides of his head and he literally had two separate conversations going on at the same time. "I'll call you back."

"Good morning, Floyd," his sexy long-haired brunet white receptionist said as she handed him his coffee in a shiny black oversized mug.

"Hold all calls," Floyd said to his personal secretary who was trying to tell him about the detectives. "You got a warrant Sherlock Holmes?" Floyd sounded almost taunting as he spoke without even making eye contact with the detectives and toyed with one of the knickknacks on his glass shelves.

"Good morning, Floyd. We are sorry to barge in like this."

"No you're not, but go ahead," Floyd said in a distain-filled tone.

"We wanted to ask you a few questions about Bohemian Johnson," the detective looked at Floyd for any clear sign of facial movement. There wasn't any.

"What about Bo," Floyd said with a flat voice and stiff poker face.

"He was murdered last night."

"So I was told earlier today."

"Oh yeah, can I ask who told you?" The detective persisted.

"I don't know, my entire summer league team, some radio people, just about every person I spoke to today has told me.

"Yeah, he was very popular. You and he didn't have any disagreements did you?"

"And with that my fine feathered friends, this meeting is over!" Floyd now sounded outright disrespectful.

"Alright, the next meeting will be at the Round House," the shorter detective barked.

"You see that picture there? That is me and the Mayor. How about that that one right there," Floyd was now pointing his index finger toward another picture on his shelf. "That's your boss the Chief. I also have cards to go along with the photos. Now which one should I call first? Oh yeah, I'm calling them both." Floyd was now smiling at what he had just said.

The detectives reluctantly left Floyd's downtown office. By the time they had reached their unmarked beat-up police car, both of their cell phones were ringing. On one phone was the Deputy Chief yelling in the phone. On the other phone was their Captain. Blair "Silk" Floyd had made good on his promise.

Chapter 23

Funny thing how it is when a person grows up in the ghetto or lives the street life. The best treatment they ever get and the most respect seems to come just after they die. All of a sudden, the whole neighborhood is building sidewalk memorials to someone who lived most of their life as a nobody in the eyes of larger society. And so it was with Bo's death, burial and beautiful service. Raheem and all their past and present team mates were attending the lavish shrine of pictures and memories from Bo's past. It was all laid out for his honor at Barbers' Hall at Board and Oxford Streets. Ironically the banquet hall was just four city blocks away from the 16th Street courts where Bo had earned his b-ball respect. Four blocks in the opposite direction was where he took his last breath.

Floyd had his office staff make all the arrangements for the re-past. The layout was top flight. Shell-fish, free alcohol, top of the line champagne. Floyd brought the Championship Trophy in a made it as if it were a winner's party. The owners of the Hall had laid out prime rib and huge Pacific Prawns. The DJ played hip hop music for the young crowd. Before long the morbid feeling of death was no more. Word got out that Raheem Porter was having a party at the Hall and teenaged girls, young women along with neighborhood chicks and college babes alike all began to line up out front.

"Go ahead and open the second and third floors, I got it," Floyd told Mr. Jake the owner and his long-time friend. Floyd made it out to be Raheem's thing after that. Raheem loved it. He and his high school buddies had simply forgotten about Bo. The party was popin.

"I can't allow these kids to drink this champagne, Floyd," the owner said.

"What can you do?" Floyd asked.

"We can make a huge sherbet punch with orange sherbet and Seven-Up.

"Good enough for me," Floyd agreed. The young adult party got pushed up two flights and the grown folks stayed with the champagne.

Although the re-past had begun as a slow requiem, it ended with the young adults and grown folk wanting for more. As the night winded down, Raheem was approached by two detectives hanging around just outside the Hall.

"Raheem, my man," One of the detectives yelled from across the street. He was standing at the edge of an adjacent parking lot. Raheem ignored the call and continued to focus on his conversation with two college students from up the block at Temple.

"We gotta yell at you home, home, home boy."

"Holla at you"

"What?"

"Holla at you, not yell at you," the other detective corrected the first on his street lingo.

"Oh yeah, we gotta holla at you homie," the short balding detective yelled from across the lot.

"Naw I'm cool," Raheem said, and continued his conversation. The detective was now crossing the street. Raheem ended his conversation and began to re-enter the Hall.

"Listen, Raheem, you know if you cross Floyd the same thing could happen to you."

"What?"

"You heard me loud and clear, son."

"Floyd ain't have shit to do with that, and you know it." Raheem was now standing in a defensive posture out of anger at the notion.

"Well how do you know that? Did you have him killed?"

"Man I'm calling my lawyer." Raheem continued and turned to go up the steps.

"You ain't got a lawyer kid, but you better get one."

Raheem swiftly walked back into the Hall in search for Floyd. As usual, Floyd was at work. He was in a far booth on his Blue Tooth talking and texting simultaneously. As soon as he spotted Raheem he redirected his energy. "I'll call you back; Raheem, what's the problem?"

"Man, these cops was just saying crazy stuff about you and Bo. That I could be next if I crossed you. Did I kill Bo and all kinds of stuff." Raheem was babbling uncontrollably.

"Slow down, have a seat. Start from the beginning but slowly. Now what did they say to you?" Floyd calmly asked but his language was very deliberate.

"First they kept calling me, but I was talking to some college girls. Then the little one said if I cross you, that I could be next."

"Okay, and what did you say in return."

"I asked what you trying to say, Floyd ain't have nothin to do with Bo getting killed."

"Then what did they say?"

"How could I know, did I kill Bo? Then I said I'm calling my lawyer."

"What happened next after you said that," Floyd finally said.

"He said that he knew I didn't have a lawyer but that I better get one."

"Well then, I guess we better get one then or maybe two," Floyd said with a smile as he put his arms around Raheem's shoulders and headed toward the door....

Chapter 24

"Hi Reheem," Tammy said as she entered the new Porter household.

"Hey Tammy, Whats up?"

"This is really nice, I love how secluded the house is from the road and the trees towering over the back beyond the yard."

"Yeah, my grandmother said that's what sold her on it," Raheem responded as he eyed Tammy in all her beauty.

"You got your pre-SAT exam today and then if you're a good boy I got a real surprise," Tammy said with a full tooth smile.

"Oh yeah," Raheem looked excited.

"Hello," Mother Porter said.

"This is my grandmother."

"Hi, I'm Tammy; I'm Raheem's assistant slash manager unofficially."

"I'm Mother Porter, everybody calls me Mother," Mother Porter said and then continued. "Come on and eat before you go.

"Okay by me," Raheem said and headed toward the kitchen. Tammy smiled and followed while having a light-hearted conversation with Mother Porter about the house. The air in the kitchen was heavy with the unmistakable scent of pork bacon and fried catfish breaded with cornmeal. Cheese hominy grits were steaming beside and a bowl of buttermilk waffle batter was waiting in a bowl.

"I have both pork bacon and turkey bacon. Raheem's new diet calls for turkey or fish everything. I don't understand it; a growing boy should learn to eat like a man!" Mother complained as she made Tammy and Raheem fresh waffles from the twin flip-style waffle iron. Mother then laid out two different syrups from warming bowls on the back of the stove. After serving the waffles she gave Raheem the ceramic cup with melted butter and a bowl of fresh strawberries and blue berries.

"Wow, do you cook like this every day?" Tammy asked as she kept one eye on the waffle iron.

"Been doing it every day for 50 years. Started when I was just a girl. Then for my husband and children and now for my grandson. Suspect I'll be doing it for my great grand-kids too," she said as Keema and Kia came to the table.

"We got company," Kia said. Then Keema turned to Tammy, "You Raheem's girlfriend?"

"No, and mind your business," Raheem barked back at Keema.

"My name is Tammy."

"Hi Tammy, I'm Kia."

"And I'm Keema; nice shoes and that bag is nice too," Keema said.

"What kind of bag is that Tammy?" Keema asked.

"It's a Birken," Tammy stated with a smile.

"Nana, I want a pocketbook like that."

"Yeah, well you had better go to college and get a good job to pay for it," Mother Porter said while beginning to plate up food for Kia and Keema.

Raheem and Tammy were finishing up when Tammy stood up from the table. Both Kia and Keema eyed her entire ensemble. They were very aware of Tammy's very expensive attire.

"Girrrl, that bag cost some money," Keema stated after the two girls figured Tammy was out of ear shot."

"Yeah, I know and her shoes too," Kia quickly added.

"Shoot, she must be getting down for hers."

"Alright, that's enough," Mother Porter barked.

"I'm ready to go back to bed after all that food," Tammy jokingly said to Raheem as the two headed toward her car. "Are you driving?"

"Hell yeah!" Raheem said as he ran toward the driver's side door and then back tracking once he remembered to open the door for Tammy like a gentleman.

"Thank you Mr. Raheem," Tammy sweetly said in her girlish voice...

***

What's up with these two bozos bothering my player about Bo's death? Evidently he was involved with some sort of drug activity," Floyd said into his office phone fully aware of the possibility of his phone being tapped.

"Yeah, well, let the process take its course. Everyone is a suspect until things work and weed people out," the lawyer on the other end of Floyd's phone responded.

"Raheem's no thug, Joe, and everybody knows that. So why in the world would they be bothering him about this?"

"Floyd, the way I see it, he and Bo were like brothers so if Bo was involved in some dirty business, Raheem would have clearly known about it. Maybe he knew the essential players involved even if he had nothing to do with the actions." Then the lawyer continued, "So let the detectives ask all their questions and then move on. Me and Dan will accompany him down to the Round House Headquarters to make sure that things don't get rough."

"Sounds good. I'll make contact with Raheem after his testing is over later this afternoon. Then I'll call you back for the scheduled meeting."

"Sounds like a plan to me." With that, the two hung up. Floyd rocked back in his high-backed leather chair. He spun around and looked at the view to Center City and his unobstructed view of City Hall with the William Penn statue. To Floyd, the clear view meant freedom. The higher up he went, meant that he was much closer to the American Dream. White picket fence, wife, kids, dog. All bullshit! His American Dream was a total unobstructed view of the City of Philadelphia from his office. From river to river, he wanted to be able to see it all. This was the view of real men with wealth and power...

Chapter 25

"I had a date with Tammy, man," Raheem protested.

"Yeah, well, we need to put a stop to this harassment. The surefire way to do that is to give them this interview. You don't have nothing to hide, so why not?" With those quick words, Floyd hung up. Raheem looked at the two lawyers and said, "Alright, let's do this thing."

The three headed to 8th and Race. The notorious Round House. Many have entered on their own free will never to have seen the streets again. To walk into the Round House for an interview with the homicide detectives was utterly ridiculous. Everyone on the street understood this. Even the bright green-eyed Raheem knew it was bad news. So why in the world didn't Floyd understand that?

"Thank you for coming in Joe. Dan, how have you been?

"I'm fine, Frank," the three all knew each other very well. They had participated in hundreds of homicide investigations as well as trials. The level of respect was evident on all sides. This was both good and bad for Raheem.

"Let's get started, shall we," the lead detective, Frank Delback said. Raheem was sitting in an small interrogation room; everything in the room was painted white except the large mirror in front of the rectangular metal table. He towered up from his chair as he sat tall and glanced at himself in the two-way mirror. He noticed the small video camera in one corner of the room and that there was a tiny red light shining at the top of the camera. Raheem figured that he was being watched at that very moment. He shrugged and turned to stare at the edge of the empty table in front of him. He folded his hands almost as if he was engaged in prayer, then he quickly unfolded them and simply stretched out his large hands with his palms flat on the table. He sat alone. Then the door of the room snapped open and one of his two lawyers walked into the interrogation room.

"Raheem, who is Moop?"

"He's my friend and team mate, Why?" Raheem asked sounding very innocent. Just then the detective walked in with his short angry partner.

"Interviewing Raheem Porter, time and date noted. Minor is accompanied by official counsel. Okay Raheem, I'm Detective Delback and this is Detective Johnson. Are you under the influence of any drugs or alcohol at this time?"

"No I am not," Raheem responded in a solid tone.

"Are you here on your own free will?" Raheem looked at the lawyer to his right. The lawyer nodded. Raheem responded to the question, "Yes I am."

"Did you know Bohemian Johnson, AKA Bo?"

"Yes I did."

"And how were you two acquainted?"

"We were friends since elementary school"

"Were you aware that Bo had been killed?"

"Yes."

"And how did you come to find that out?"

"I got a call from Moop the morning after it happened." Raheem began to shift in his seat a bit.

"Where were you on the night that Bo was killed?"

Before he responded, Raheem twisted up his face a bit showing his annoyance with the slow progression of the questions, "Before or after our championship game?"

"After the game of course," the detective now asking the questions said with a sharp tone.

"I went home."

"Home as in 9th and Indiana Streets?"

"No, I went to my Grandmom's in Chester County.

"Yeah, that's what I keep hearing about. The big house out in Kennett Square. How did you grandmother get that?"

"Don't answer that!" The lawyer quickly piped in. "You keep that up and we're outta her, Frank. It was a sharp rebuke but the detective refused to even acknowledge it as he quickly continued, almost cutting the lawyer off at the end of his statement.

"Who is Moop?"

"He is a friend and team mate."

How long have you known him?"

"Probably just as long as I've known Bo."

"So you two are pretty tight?

"Yes I would say that."

"Do you think Moop would lie to you in any way or try to hurt you?

"Where is this going Frank? I mean it, we got one foot out that got damn door!" The lawyer was beginning to sound very serious with his threat to leave the interview room.

"Let me ask the kid some questions Joe."

"Would Moop lie about you, what do you think?"

"I would say no," Raheem slowly responded.

"So if he told us that he thought you might have somehow been behind having Bo killed, that would be the truth?"

"Me? He's the one who told me that Bo got killed in the first place," Raheem now was visibly upset. He squirmed a little in his seat, slouched down and then straightened up to sit tall again.

"I didn't say that you killed him yourself. I said that it was possible that you were behind somehow in the murder of Bo."

"Why in the world would I want Bo dead, he was my best friend?"

"Oh I don't know. Maybe because he had threatened to go to the NCAA on you."

"He never did that." The back-and-forth pace of questions and answers was now picking up speed in a noticeable way that seemed to be making Raheem's lawyer a bit tense. It was almost as if his brain was having trouble figuring out where this process was heading in time to help out his client.

"Or because he had been having sex with both your cousin and your little sister."

"Enough Frank, God dammit," the lawyer finally cried out but it seemed to make absolutely no difference.

Raheem's face dropped with shock and surprise, "Sex with my cousin and my sister? He wouldn't do that to me; he wouldn't do no shit like that! You guys are making up all this. It's a bunch of shit."

"It's possible that he may have even forced himself on you little sister from the way I hear it." The detective now gabbing the bull by the horns and going in for the kill.

"What? Cmon man, I'm otta here!"

"Sit down, you're not going anywhere." Both detectives took a defensive position by moving to block the door. Raheem was now showing all of his anger as he grabbed Detective Delback by the collar and, with very little effort, slugged him, sending him flying across the room. Detective Johnson jumped out of Raheem's way and began to bang on the mirror.

"Calm down Raheem," the lawyer yelled in vain. Raheem tried the door but it was locked from the outside. A few seconds passed and the steel door swung open. Several plain and uniformed officers stormed the room and tackled the giant teen.

"Cuffum Jim," the lawyer could hear one officer saying but the small room was now flooded and out of control. One idiot cop shot his taser gun in the pileup and ended up shocking the entire pile of men.

"Bob you fucking moron, why the hell would you do that?" The office Captain yelled at the clown who had tased the group. "Get the fuck outta here, go home you fool."

After a few minutes the ruckus was over. Raheem no longer looked young and innocent. He had a bloody nose. His eyes were bloodshot red and he had a split lower lip that was dripping a small stream of blood down on his torn tee-shirt. His massive shoulders had veins bulging out up into his thick neck.

"Where are you taking him? Now both the lawyers were protesting but nobody seemed to be listening. There was too much testosterone and adrenaline flowing in the small room.

"He's getting booked for aggravated assault," the Captain yelled. Raheem's booking photo wasn't that of the good-looking athletic phenom. It was a picture of a huge, blood thirsty African American criminal. Raheem's photo now fit the image of America's worst nightmare...

Chapter 26

"What?" Floyd was yelling in a way that was not characteristic of his usually cool and collected self.

"Floyd listen."

"No, you listen you stupid motherfucker! You and your jack-legged partner had better find a way to get my boy out of this jam or I'm going to show you what being in trouble really means!" Floyd hung up the phone and pushed out of the office.

Raheem was rushed off to the county jail. He had just turned 17 years old. Being a minor should have sent him directly to the juvenile detention center, however, because of his massive size and the nature of his crime being aggravated assault on 10 police officers, as was well as being involved in a gruesome murder investigation, he was screwed. The magistrate sent him directly to the big house county jail. "The Creek," as it was affectionately named for the constant stream of blood that ran down the inmate cell blocks on a daily basis from turf wars. Yes, this particular facility was technically for juveniles 21 and under. But this place housed the absolute worst of the worst.

"Floyd, come on man, you gotta get me outta her," Raheem pled from behind the glass partition."

"I'm working on it. That fucking magistrate denied your bail because of the assault on the police. He said that young people today have no respect for authority and he wanted you to get the message loud and clear. What the fuck went wrong?"

"I don't know Floyd. Something fucked up is happening. They was saying crazy shit and I just lost it. I was only trying to leave."

"Saying crazy shit like what?"

"That Bo was gonna report me to the NCAA and that he was fucking my little sister and cousin."

"What?"

"Yeah, then he tried to say that Bo raped Kia!"

"Where did they get a story like that?"

"Moop!"

"Moop?"

"Yeah, Moop told them that Bo was crossing me in every way possible so I somehow had him killed. That's when I snapped and tried to leave. When they tried to stop me, I think I tossed one of them across the room. The door was locked from the outside so I couldn't get out man!" Raheem was crying.

"Calm down, Heem. I'm gonna deal with this," Floyd said in a calm voice. At the same time he was using his free hand in a settle down whoa motion.

"Then about thirty of them jumped me. They tased me, punched me in my nose, stomped me! What did I do to deserve this Floyd?"

"I know, I know. I'm gonna sue the entire police department, you'll see." Floyd sounded convincing. "Give me a day or two; I'm going to City Hall. I'm gonna see if we can get this fixed before the newspapers get it.

Just then, Mother Porter, Keisha, Keema and Kia all rushed into the visiting area. "Oh my Lord, they done hurt my baby," Mother Porter cried out.

"Keep it down Please," the guard on duty by the door said without looking in the direction of the family.

"Are you alright?" Keisha was the first on the phone but Mother Porter snatched it out of her hands.

"What did they do Baby?"

"I'm cool Nana." Raheem was wiping his face to show a sign of bravery in front of his family.

"Are you eating, did they feed you, they not starving you are they baby?"

"No Nana, I'm fine, really. Floyd and the lawyers are handling everything I promise." Raheem sounded strong and convincing. Keema was pulling on the phone. Mother Porter reluctantly let go and began to sob.

"What's up Killa?" Keema jokingly said.

"Cool out Keema wit the dumb shit," Raheem responded.

"Naw, you alright?"

"Yeah, I'm good. I just need to get outta here. I gotta ask you something," Raheem sounded very focused and serious now.

"What?"

"Why didn't you tell me about you and Bo?"

"It wasn't nothing to really tell Raheem," Keema looked up at her big cousin.

"Are you telling me the truth?"

"It was just a little fling that's' all," Keema said as tears began to fall down her face. "When they gonna let you out?"

"Soon, now let me talk to Kia," Raheem said sharply and sounding a bit rude after hearing what he had dreaded.

"Hi Ra."

"What's up little one," Raheem affectionately called his little sister.

"You know what I'm gonna ask right," Raheem said.

"No, I don't know," Kia responded very swiftly.

"Did Bo rape you?"

"What. Hell no, who told you that? I'll, I'll!" Kia said as her face seemed to break up with a mix of emotions.

"Naw, it's some bullshit that cops started, that's all." Raheem sounded relieved.

Kia was deep inside herself. She felt terrible for lying to her brother but she knew that she needed to protect both him and June. June wouldn't want words like that floating around about her so she was sure her secret would be safe, especially since Bo was now dead. The young

Kia was wise beyond her years. Day after day of working side-by-side with her grandmother had slowly rubbed off on her.

"Listen big Bra, you just take care of yourself inside there and hurry up home." Kia looked up at her big brother with sad eyes.

"I will Little One; I love you," Raheem said with strength. His face was firm now that his emotions were in check. This new and difficult set of circumstances was clearly a shock to the Porter Clan. Each fought for the phone to say as much as possible in the 30 minutes allotted. The thick glass separating the family just added to the stess.

The tearful goodbyes were tough but Floyd had a way of making everyone feel comfortable that he was on the case. And, in truth, he most definitely was taking care of everything. The first thing that Floyd did was fire the two lawyers who had so foolishly advised him to cooperate. He immediately hired a politically connected attorney. A true campaign contributor. "Campaign contributions have a way of opening closed doors," the wise attorney once told Blair Floyd and Floyd never forgot those words. This was Philadelphia after all and everybody understood that one has to pay to play...

***

Don't worry Floyd. Give me a few days and I'll iron this mess out."

"Thanks Dennis, I know I should have conferred with you from the start, but it was supposed to be just an interview," Floyd explained over the phone as he headed back up the Interstate highway toward his Center City office.

"Yeah well, it is what it is, so let me deal with it."

"Good enough for me Dennis." And with that the two hung up.

151

Floyd drove on the highway with the big city lights out in the distant skyline. Thoughts were racing through his head: "What the hell happened? In only 24 hours the entire complexion of the game had changed." He thought briefly of Moop who seemed to be the cause of all this new turbulence. Floyd would see to it very soon that Moop would get a little talking to. There was absolutely no reason for Raheem's name to have come up in such a mess like this.

Chapter 27

"Well, I never said nothing about it to nobody."

"Nobody June? You swear?"

"Nobody, I swear. I don't want nobody knowing some shit like that. I ain't never even had you before, why would I want people to know that Bo had you?"

"He didn't have me June, he raped me!" Kia shot back quickly.

"And you do have me. You have my heart!" Kia eyes began to tear up.

"Come here, I apologizes Ma."

"Why would you talk like that?" Kia was now in June's arms. June was with her, holding her, but his thoughts were off in another direction...

Chapter 28

"What we have here is a simple miscarriage of justice that escalated into police brutality. To circumvent their action of brutality, the Philadelphia Police Department and several members of the force have charged the young, law abiding Raheem Porter with felony assault. This young man is an A student and a highly sought after community helper. His entire community has vigorously stood behind him during these few days of trouble." The lawyer was speaking with Raheem by his side, sporting a neck brace and a black eye. There were some 70 neighbors surrounding them.

"Well what do you have to say about the murder of Bohemian Johnson?" One reporter shouted out.

"We have nothing to say about it. It was a sad day for his family as well for Raheem. They were childhood friends for Christ's sake. What's your name? Who do you represent to ask a young kid such a hideous question like that. You should lose your license to be a journalist. No more questions, no more questions." With that, the lawyer saw a chance to scurry away with the ball back in Raheem's court. The two hopped in his car and drove to his downtown office for a quick debriefing and discussion.

The very polished and politically well-connected offices of McDugle and McGuire shined like a beacon of light over the Philadelphia skyline. Dennis McDugle, the son of the last and very powerful Dan "Danny Boy" McDugle of the now defunct U.U.M.A.--United Union Members of America. He was an honor graduate of the prestigious Georgetown Law School. Tall, very handsome, athletically built middle-aged white American Dennis McDugle wore it well. He was one of Philadelphia's most successful lawyers as well as one of Pennsylvania's largest political financial contributors. Simply put, "When Dennis calls, people not only answer, they dish out the favors. That being said, a small matter such as Raheem Porter was simply a little favor for a much bigger client such as the now deep-pocketed Blair Floyd.

"Listen Raheem, I don't know how this situation escalated to this magnitude but let me give you some free advice. You stay away from anyone who is involved in any funny business. And that could mean anyone. You got me!"

"Yes sir," Raheem replied.

"You got a bright future ahead of you. Don't go mucking it up with all this street malarkey. I don't need your business, you hear."

"Yes sir."

"I've got plenty of business coming in from real criminals. Guys who commit crime for a living and trust me, baby, you ain't one of um. You got that?"

"Yes sir."

"Now let me talk to you grandmother."

"Okay, thank you Mr. Dennis," the grateful Raheem offered his right hand out to shake.

"Atta boy," the lawyer said as he grasped Raheem's large palm.

Ms Porter entered the room with the stern look of an angry mother ready to fight. As the lawyer explained the circumstances, she loosened up.

"He's not in any trouble, Ms Porter; in fact we may have a bit of a small case here. A settlement probably once I rattle the cage."

"How small," Mother Porter asked and her shrewd business savvy did not go unnoticed.

"Well, they did beat the kid up. I got ahold of the tape before they erased it. I had it played on the news once already. Both the Mayor and the Chief are calling like roosters to have me stop this campaign. So, in the interest of justice and all that good stuff, I'd say 200. I'll ask for 400, after all Raheem is an A student and he'll need college money."

Mother Porter never changed her facial expression, not one bit as she sternly asked, "And your slice?"

"I'll ask for lawyer fees separate. I'll get it; nobody wants to fight old Dennis. Especially when tapes and kids are involved. Okay we got that covered, now listen to me carefully. Here is my card. Any funny business, any at all, you call me."

"Thank you Mr. Dennis, thank you so kindly."

"It's my pleasure." The two shook hands and Mother Porter left with her grandson in tow just as if he were a little boy.

The entire Porter family was driven home by Tammy. The mood was much better than it had been for the past few nights. Tammy was simply happy to be of service to her young friend Raheem. And he was very happy to be free. Although he had only spent two nights in the county jail, it had felt like a lifetime. "I ain't never, never, ever committing no crimes," Raheem said as the entire car cracked up in laughter.

"You see why I always say be a good boy."

"Yes Nana, I'm gone always listen too. Raheem is a good boy," she said as he grinned toward his Nana.

"Raheem is a punk, that's what he is! One little night in jail." Keema said grinding her cousin up.

"Shut up girl," Raheem said as he reclined in the passenger seat and got some rest on the ride home. It seemed like a much more sunny and beautiful ride at the moment for the young Raheem...

Chapter 29

Raheem and his family pulled into the shrubbery surrounding the driveway. Mother Porter and the girls immediately got out of the car while Raheem and Tammy talked remained and talked for a while.

"Are you alright?" Tammy appeared very somber and concerned.

"Yeah, I'm good, you know that," Raheem said with an air of bravado. The two got out of the car and slowly walked toward the front door as they continued to chat. It had been a long few days for the young Raheem but Tammy had a way of making him feel at ease. With his SATs now behind him, Raheem could now focus on his senior year of high school and his fundamentals in basketball.

As Raheem walked into the entrance of the kitchen, he heard the familiar sound of a male voice. As he came closer, he spotted Moop sitting in the kitchen softly speaking to Mother Porter.

"Hey Moop, I didn't know you were here."

"Yeah I've been here for a while waiting for you to show," Moop said as he pushed a chair out from under the kitchen table for his long legs to stand. The two friends hugged

"Moop, tell Raheem the good news," Mother Porter stated as she prepared to warm up some leftovers.

"What Moop, you getting married?"

"No, stupid, I'm headed to NC."

"A Tarheel? Really?"

"Yeah, and hopefully Mill and Malik."

"Yeah, when did all this happen?"

"Hey man, you've been away in prison!" "Yeah, it feels like that. Where are them two fools anyway, don't they know I'm out?"

Just then, a new SUV pulled into the driveway. Both Mill and Malik jumped out of the shiny truck and moved quickly toward the house.

"Yo, anybody home?"

"Yo man, we just was rappin bout yall, what's up?" The four friends embraced like old times.

"NC?"

"Oh you heard huh," Malik said sarcastically.

"Yeah of course I heard fool. I'm ready to put on some baby blue."

"You should Heem."

"Man I gave Floyd my word about Kansas. I can't turn back on him now."

"Hey, yall go eat, I need to holla at Moop for a minute. The two friends hopped up immediately at the word "eat". Raheem looked at Moop for what seemed an eternity.

"What give Moop?"

"What bro?"

"Did you tell them cops I had Bo killed?"

"What, why in the world would I say that? You trippin?"

"How about my little sister Moop?"

"Kia?"

"Yeah, Kia."

"What about Kia?"

"Them cops said you told them that Bo raped her so I had him killed."

"What?"

"Yeah, that's how the fight started with me and the whole damn force stomping me out like this, then charging me with assault."

"Heem, Kia is like my little sister, if that would have happened, I would have dealt with Bo myself and you know that man."

Raheem gave these words of Moop some thought. He was right, but why would or who would pass on such a ruthless lie like that? Rape? They could have simply said that he was messing around with Kia and that in itself would have been enough to upset Raheem, but rape?

"I guess you're right Moop. You are like my brother. I'm sorry that I had to ask you all those questions."

"It ain't nothing Heem man, I love you Bro." The two hugged and walked into the kitchen to eat like men.

Just on the other side of the adjacent hallway in the kitchen apron, Mother Porter stood. After the two finished when joined them all in their new kitchen and served her grandson and his childhood friends. They ate, laughed, and ate some more. As the evening started to grow old, Mother Porter called for Kia to lend her a hand in the kitchen. As Kia passed her in the hall, Mother Porter playfully swatted her granddaughter with the dish towel. She hugged Mill and Malik goodbye.

"You boys be good, you hear. Especially you Mill."

"Yes Mother." They both said as they headed out the door. Moop hugged Mother Porter and thanked her for everything.

"You just do like Nana says, and everything well be fine. You understand me Moop?"

"Yes Mam." With that, Mother Porter shot Moop that all-knowing eye of hers. Raheem saw the look. A look he'd seen many times before but this was a bit different. This look was almost scary. Mother Porter turned and headed toward the kitchen. She began to work side-by-side with her granddaughter. Raheem walked to the entrance and watched. On this day his usually small grandmother could have been ten feet tall. Raheem could feel power and energy radiating from and around her body. Raheem looked on with amazement and then caught himself.

"You still hungry baby?

"No I'm not Nana." He pondered a bit more while his young inquisitive mind bounced from subject to subject. "How in God's name could all of his friends have accomplished committing to one university in such a short period of time? It was utterly impossible to do. Unless, unless they had been previously working on it all along?"

"Nana?"

"Yes baby."

"Would you be upset with me if I decided to go to NC instead of Kansas?"

"Why would I be upset? NC is a beautiful school to attend. I could make sure all of you are in one house following your freshman year. It would really put my mind at ease, you being with friends and family. Nothing is more important Raheem."

Raheem thought for a few seconds more. He was leaning up against the frame of the doorway with his right hand on his hip. "It's settled then, I'll be a Tarheel next year.

The night came to a peaceful end. Mother Porter talked with Kia as the two got ready to retire.

"You don't ever have to be afraid to talk with your Nana."

"I know Nana."

Raheem Porter lay in his bed and slowly went over the entire week. He thought about Bo and why someone would kill him. Then he went over all the detective had said to him and why? Floyd. Floyd had been a very aggressive player in all of this. He controlled all the strings in the band. Or did he?

Raheem began to drift off to talk to the father figure who was always in the back of his mind. He saw himself sitting in a barber's chair. The constant hum of the clippers in his ears relaxed him. "You too dad?"

The imaginary shadow in his mind clearly answered, "Yeah, they relax me also."

"You know I chose the Tar Heels?"

"Yeah, I know your grandmother decided that's where you would go."

"No I decided to go there."

"Yeah, your grandmother decided for you."

"Dad, why do you keep saying that?"

"Saying what?

"That Nana made the choice for me."

"Mother Porter makes all the decisions, didn't you know that?"

Kia and her Grandmom had meandered toward the rear of the house to lock up. Mother Porter opened the patio door to let Gonzo inside. "Calm down Gonzo, calm down or your ass is going back outside!" Mother raised her voice just enough for Gonzo to get the point. He sat down and looked up at the family matriarch.

"You be good and Nan's got them snacks you like." Gonzo had a high pitched whine. "Now go on upstairs." Gonzo obeyed. Mother turned and hugged her granddaughter who had been intently watching her Nana. She kissed her forehead and quietly said in Kia's ear, "Nana knows everything." Kia did not respond. She and her grandmother climbed the stairs. Mother Porter went left to her room while Kia went to the right.

When Mother Porter approached her locked bedroom door, Gonzo was waiting patiently. Mother Porter pulled the key from around her neck and unlocked the heavy hardwood door.

"Go on," Gonzo entered the bedroom and Mother followed. She closed the door behind her and locked it. Mother Porter's bedroom was now just as clean and neat as it had been on 9th Street. This bedroom was only much bigger. She chose to purchase a new bed, queen-sized, with four posts. Her armoire was the same one that she had owned for almost 30 years. She had a new television at the foot of the bed. Gonzo would watch it much more than she did. Her bed was flanked on each side by a nightstand with a small brushed nickel lamp. There were two books on a little shelf next to the side of the bed where she most often ended up sleeping. *Beloved* by Toni Morrison and a much thicker book entitled *The 1000 Points of Light: Mothers of Darkness*.

On the far side of the bed, almost totally shoved underneath the bed, was a large black travel bag. Mother unzipped the bag and slowly but methodically stacked the hundred dollar bills into her own new safe that was in the back of her closet. Once she completed the task she reached for her large book. Inside was an envelope with her grandson's name at the end. Mother Porter had already committed Raheem to NC about two weeks earlier. It would soon be official...

Special Thanks

To my agent Marcellus Autrey for your tireless work seeing this project come to completion while demonstrating such a professional manner throughout the entire development.

Also, to my Aunt Gloria for always being there for me when I needed you the most.

Thank you

Coming Soon!

North I-95

Money Never Sleeps

Carlito Ewell

North I-95
Money Never Sleeps
Carlito Ewell

Chapter 1

Orlando/Prison

Once settled in at the El Conquistador's plaza guest suites on the top floors, there was a knock at the door. Clayton Jones quickly rushed to see who it was. He was still feeling a bit nervous. It was Reina, wife of Columbian drug cartel head Orlando Garcia. She had her children in tow which made Clayton relax momentarily.

"Hola Clayton, Orlando is waiting for you," her words spilled out quickly while hugging and kissing him on the cheeks. Two older women in blue nurse's outfits and a large man were present in the hall; they all filed in. Another man quickly showed up and stood outside the hotel room door. He never even looked at Clayton. Securing the door was his only concern. "Typical drug lord stuff," Clayton thought. He was comforted by the feeling that between the guard in the hallway and the nurses inside, his family was safe.

At the elevator, another Colombian bodyguard appeared when the doors opened. "Hola Mr. Clayton, Orlando is waiting."

"Got damn, did Orlando bring the entire Colombian Army," Clayton said out loud this time.

"Que?" the bodyguard did not speak English at all.

"Bien, bien, bien amigo." Clayton quickly responded to the man while flagging his right hand as if to say, "Nothing, forget about it."

After a short drive, the men were at the golf course. Clayton did not golf so he reasoned that the day would be a long one.

Clayton was right. After he and Orlando hugged, a jubilant Orlando flashed his toothy smile, "How was your flight my friend? Orlando showed a joy that seemed very genuine to Clayton. Orlando didn't bother to hide his feelings; he admired this young man and freely showed him. A man of Orlando's stature didn't have to hide his feelings; if he liked someone he showed it and if not, well...

The two played golf all morning. They talked about golf, and played more golf. Orlando was really enjoying himself. He was beating the shit out of Clayton who didn't even know how to keep score.

"Clayton, I love this game!" Orlando shouted as he sank a 25 foot putt. "You love it too, yes?" Orlando said as he roughly patted Clayton on his shoulder with his large mitt of a hand. He began walking toward the golf cart to start heading toward the next hole.

"Yeah, I love it too, Orlando," Clayton sarcastically said as he plopped into the passenger seat of the gold cart. How else would he respond to the man who ran the Colombian drug cartel? For the moment all was well. Clayton took time to enjoy the fact that the air seemed clear and Orlando appeared to be in the best mood that Clayton had ever seen. All of this might have been true but Clayton had been in the game long enough to know that the complexion could change at a moment's notice. Just because things seemed to be going well between the two had very little to do with business. Business trumped all else. Business was more important than any feelings that the two men may have had for one another. Business is lord and ruler over life and death and that's just how it was.

The two played one more hole which Orlando birdied. "I'm the best!" Orlando cried out with both arms raised and fists clenched. Clayton unceremoniously threw up his right hand and shook his head as if to agree and mockingly congratulate his elder mentor.

"Yes you are Orlando, you are the best."

"Maybe you are better at chess, yes, Clayton?" Orlando said in a gloating tone as he roughly patted Clayton's shoulder and stepped into the golf cart. Clayton threw his club in the back of the cart, missing the golf bag by such a distance that when Orlando pulled off, the club fell to the ground. One of the four men following jumped out of their cart and grabbed it. The group moved on to the next hole, leaving that loyal servant to walk back to the clubhouse.

After showering, steaming and taking a quick sauna the men took their lunch and drinks in the smoking room. The chess board awaited. Clayton sat down to eat first, ignoring Orlando's challenge.

"Hambriento, Clayton?"

Clayton just continued to dig into his food.

"Why am I here, Orlando? You know all the stuff I have going on back in the states. My brother, Mike, is facing two death sentences. He's being railroaded by some politicians for the sake of the waterfront development in Chester, Pennsylvania. My number two man in Atlanta just got indicted by the Feds down there, and I got a pending war building up in Chester over M.T.'s project."

Orlando looked at the large chess board and then back at Clayton. He had now joined his friend at the lunch table and the elaborate spread. Clayton was rambling on about his troubles while Orlando looked over the spread for something in particular. Once the kingpin seemed to have found what he'd been searching for, he began to eat. Clayton continued on and on, all the while Orlando shook his head up and down while chewing. He reached in to the center of the table for the large antique wine bottle, pulled the cork off the top and poured the deep dark red wine into his glass; he then poured a glass for Clayton.

"You're going to have trouble building with Ramonsito too my friend," Orlando said while shoveling a fork full of shrimp and saffron-colored rice into his mouth.

"Who the fuck is Ramonsito, and why do I have a beef with him?"

Orlando just continued to chew his food and shrugged his shoulders, then finally spoke. "You know the gentleman; you destroyed his business in New York with your cheap prices."

"What, the Dominicans?" Clayton sounded almost surprised. "They've been there for 20 years now. How did I destroy their business? Plus, I used to buy from them and gave them the chance to buy from me. I never heard of no Ramonsito." Clayton was no longer eating; he was now pissed about all of this new information and the possible trouble crashing down around him.

"That's because Ramonsito is in Santo Domingo," Orlando said as he looked through the seafood paella for chunks of lobster to dip into his melted butter on the side.

"Then why the hell am I concerned about him?" Clayton almost yelled.

Orlando smiled each time he gathered a new piece of lobster tail, then finally said, "Because he has power, Medellin backs him up. We will take care of him, you will need to take care of Harlem and take over."

"I'm not moving to Harlem!" Clayton protested.

"Hundreds of millions in Harlem; it's either that or Miami, you can do it, Clayton."

"Miami?"

"You have to do one or the other; we need you. You are the best Clayton, and I assured the Board that you would agree."

"Why would you do that, I don't want to leave my area, Orlando. North I-95, that's my area, that's what I'm good at. California––trouble, Texas––trouble, Miami––trouble, New York even more trouble." Clayton was speaking at an insane pace. "Listen I was hoping to get out of the business soon, if not today."

Orlando stopped eating. He put his fork down. "Langosta mas, y, matequilla," Orlando told the waiter standing to his rear and right. The man immediately ran off. "This is a lifetime appointment you have, Clayton Jones. Very few men have had the privilege to sit and eat with any man on the Board, let alone Orlando Garcia. You have become extremely comfortable with me, Clayton Jones." While the men spoke another waiter came with the lobster and melted butter. A few seconds later a bodyguard pushing a cart with a tray covered by a silver dome came over to Clayton.

"No, gracias," Clayton said.

Orlando looked at the guard. He lifted the dome. Clayton jumped back in his seat. The head of the first waiter was on the tray. The silver platter where the head was placed

Biography

Carlton "Carlito" Ewell

Carlton Ewell is a *lifer* in the State Correctional Institution, Somerset, Pennsylvania. He is the real deal, having lived life in the streets and now paying for some of the choices that he made as a young man and rising drug lord in the Philadelphia area. He grew up in Philadelphia, PA, attended the Milton Hershey School in Hershey, Pennsylvania before serving in the U.S. Air Force. He began writing seriously after being encouraged by a Villanova University college professor teaching a creative writing course being offered at Graterford State Prison in Pennsylvania. He has published several short essays. *Ain't No Place Safe* is his first novel. It is a fictionalized memoir inspired by one of his cellmates at Graterford. He continues to write novels based on his real life experiences and those of his contemporaries.

North I-95
By

Carlito Ewell

Contact Information:
Carlito Ewell
c/o John Kovach
6 E. Possum Hollow Rd.
Wallingford, PA 19086
610-566-4446
KovachJ@chc.edu

Printed in the United States
By Bookmasters